T[illegible]ORD'S CHANGE

Brian Clark

Telford's Change

ADAPTED BY
Jim Hawkins

CORGI BOOKS
A DIVISION OF TRANSWORLD PUBLISHERS LTD

TELFORD'S CHANGE
A CORGI BOOK 0 552 10978 9

First publication in Great Britain

PRINTING HISTORY
Corgi edition published 1979

This book is set in 10pt Times

Corgi Books are published by Transworld Publishers Ltd.,
Century House, 61–63 Uxbridge Road,
Ealing, London, W.5.
Made and printed in Great Britain by
Hunt Barnard Printing Ltd., Aylesbury, Bucks.

Telford's Change

Chapter One

Mark Telford pushed aside the plastic tray of warm uneaten food, as the plane dropped down through the clouds towards Brussels. He was trying to clear his mind of the complications which had surrounded his talks in Frankfurt, and think rather of the coming meeting with Monsieur Dupont, for which he was ill prepared. If only his flight to London had not been late, Philip Haslet, the Senior General Manager of the International Division, would not have reached him at Frankfurt and sent him off for yet another continental business lunch. Sometimes Mark wondered whether Knight's Bank ought not to be renamed Flight's Bank. Mark looked down at Belgium and wished it was Surrey. He sighed quickly. The woman in the seat next to him turned her head, smiled and glanced at the German newspaper on Mark's tray, folded to a long list of market prices. He smiled back at her and as a result had to listen to a brief lecture on the value of meditation.

Despite an intelligent, distinguished appearance – donnish almost – Mark was an expert at moving quickly through the ramps and tunnels of international airports. He carried his briefcase like a shield and narrowed his lips in a determined mask that caused the dazed crowds of tourists to part like the waters before Moses.

Tom Wilson was waiting at the Customs exit with a detailed brief on Manton's and Jaques Dupont. In the taxi, Mark primed himself for the interview.

Manton's: *a multi-national chemical company based in Lille, capitalised at 100 billion francs. Most important division pharmaceuticals, but the nitrogen plant in Marseilles is the third biggest in the EEC. Some stake in oil, plants in most EEC countries, but not so far in the United Kingdom. Now interested in setting up a plant in Kent . . .*

Mark turned to Wilson. 'They'll get the money from Credit France, not from us,' he said.

Wilson nodded. 'They are Manton's main bankers, but Head Office is determined we should try everything to get them away.'

Mark slipped the documents into his case and looked, without love, at passing Brussels. 'I forget how ugly it is until I come back,' he said. 'A few fine buildings set in an aspic of prestressed concrete.'

Wilson had lived in the city so long he felt like a native. 'What about the City of London?' he said.

'That proves my point,' said Mark. 'Institutions with more money than taste demonstrate it in concrete.'

They made a stop at the Dealing Room so that Mark could check the latest exchange rates before meeting Manton's Finance Director. At a vast circular desk the dealers shouted prices over the sound of continually ringing telephones. Here, all the currencies of the world met, were given voice, and weighed themselves against each other in a clamour that was full of excitement but devoid of soul. Mark thought wearily of Poe's line ' . . . the tintinnabulation of the ringing of the bells', and of the grand piano standing silent in his London house, then shrugged the moment off and returned to the taxi.

Sylvia Telford was also on the move. Philip Haslet's secretary had just telephoned to say that Mark would not be back from Germany as expected; or rather, as usual. That would leave a difficult gap in Celia's dinner party for the third – or was it the fourth? – time. Sylvia brushed through her soft fair hair and regarded herself in the hall mirror. Forty years had not damaged her fine features, but even good cosmetics and much care had not prevented just the faintest slackening of her skin. She felt a hint of resentment that whilst Mark was so often absent, time was not. Mark might see himself as a Ulysses, wresting spoils from the Gorgons of European finance, but she was a reluctant, an increasingly reluctant, Penelope.

Peter had spent most of his lunch break from school singing and playing his guitar. The strumming from above flagged and ceased. As far as Sylvia could tell, it had been a highly repetitious and unbroken thirty minute expiation of the dark gods of adolescence. Was I like that? Sylvia wondered. Or is it only this generation that confronts life with a mixture of Jacobean violence and Victorian lugubriosity?

Her son strolled down to the bottom step of the stairs and sat on it. Sylvia took her light beige coat from the hallstand and brushed a hair from the collar.

'Don't tell me,' said Peter, 'Dad's not coming home today. He's got an urgent appointment in Timbuctoo, where he's trying to finance the sale of coconuts to Eskimos.'

'Something like that. Celia will be furious. We were going there for dinner tonight.' She turned and looked at him. 'Peter?' she said, speculatively.

He shook his head. 'No mother, please. You know I hate dinner parties. In any case, I want to take Jenny skating.'

'When did you fix that up?'

Peter grinned. 'You know how it is.'

Sylvia slipped her arm into the coat. 'Well, Celia will either have to dig up another man or I'll have to come skating with you and Jenny!'

Peter rose slowly from his position and attempted to enthuse, 'Er . . . yes . . . I mean, why don't you do that? We'd enjoy having you along.'

Sylvia laughed. 'Don't overdo it Peter, or I might accept.'

They grinned understandingly at each other before she turned and opened the door.

The Arts Council Theatre Grants Committee was, like the dealers in the Brussels exchange room, considering money, trying to come to some agreement about the distribution of the small amounts it was empowered to dispense. The word 'excellence' was heard frequently, a quality which, Sylvia argued, they were accustomed to thinking of as a special attribute of large, well-funded theatres in London and the Home Counties; whereas with broader thought and more judicious grant aid they might allow it to blossom on smaller stages in Hull, Liverpool, Newcastle and other strange lands to the north of Potters Bar. Max Fielding smiled his dignified smile from the Chair, weathered the storm, and indulged her, indeed, encouraged her, whilst gently steering the money into safe harbours not too far from the watchful lighthouse of the metropolis.

When the meeting ended, or at least fractured into informal groups, Max squeezed her elbow, praised her performance, and said how much he was looking forward to being her partner at Celia's dinner. Then his silver hair disappeared amongst the crowd of committee members. Celia looked mischievously over the shoulder of a boring lady with a vulgar hat but good connections and winked at Sylvia.

Mark's lunch with Monsieur Dupont began with the usual sparring match about which language they should speak. The lobster sat between them on the table like an emblem of a long-forgotten age. Monsieur Dupont was French, from the polish on his shoes to the polish on his hair but they agreed to converse in English.

'You made good business in Germany, yes,' enquired Mr Dupont innocently.

'Yes,' said Mark. 'It was a satisfactory trip I think.'

'Who was it you said you were visiting?' Dupont continued.

Mark sipped his cool white wine, 'I didn't say.'

Monsieur Dupont lifted his glass not quite in a toast. 'No of course you didn't,' he said, 'But it was satisfactory?'

Mark nodded.

Dupont smiled knowingly across the red claws of the lobster.

'Then . . . Krantz Brothers must have been happy

with your terms.' He paused a moment before continuing, 'And Herr Streitzer strikes a hard bargain.' Dupont's smile broadened, revealing a little gold on the white mountain peaks of his teeth.

'Forgive me, Mr Telford, I am joking with you. I am the Finance Director of a very large company. It's my job to know the capital market – who is borrowing – and who is lending . . . '

'Of course,' said Mark leaning forward. 'But it's not my job to confirm or deny whether you have guessed correctly . . . '

Dupont's smile broadened still further. 'I can see,' he said, 'that I shall enjoy this lunch.' He was right, the lunch was unmarred with talk of anything as indigestible as money. The Cognac had arrived before Dupont pointed out gently that Credit France had offered very competitive terms for a loan of ten million pounds sterling.

'What?' said Mark, 'better than Banque des Credits? They're interested too, I believe?'

'Touché Monsieur.'

But Dupont did admit that they had operations in many countries and financial dealings with many banks in France, Germany, Belgium and Italy. Dupont then made that characteristically French gesture which consists in pursing the lips and proffering the palms. It had occurred to them, he suggested, that it might be good business to approach an English bank outside the group with which they usually worked.

As the Cognac gave its benevolent sting to their throats they parried interest rates. Mark suggested ten million pounds at fifteen per cent, and Dupont laughed, telling him that the interest rate he had in mind was perhaps nearer one or two per cent. Mark suggested drily that, had he already found that sort of money at that sort of interest, they would not be having either the lunch or the conversation. 'I shall have to discuss this with my colleagues in London,' said Mark, 'and then we will come back to you with an offer. You have a site in Kent, I believe?'

'That's right. Not far from Dover.'

'Have you bought it yet?' Mark asked.

Again Dupont shrugged. 'Not yet. We have an option

to buy, conditional on permission to build.'

Mark smiled towards the ceiling and then dropped his gaze to meet Dupont's before saying, 'I should think that's a mere formality.'

Despite the excellence of the lunch, in particular the lobster, he was feeling a pang of indigestion. Monsieur Dupont had indeed been agreeable company but Mark was pleased when the moment arrived that released him from the meeting. He shook hands with Dupont and went out to the taxi that Tom Wilson had ordered.

'Will we get it do you think?' asked Wilson as he opened the door to the taxi.

'No, I shouldn't think so. We'd have to come up with something very good to woo him away from his Bank's U.K. partner.' Mark smiled, 'Still, the lobster *was* very good and it was nice to see you again. I'll keep you informed.'

He turned and waved as the taxi carried him away from Tom Wilson and away from Brussels.

Mark telephoned Head Office from the airport and told Philip Haslet that he thought it unlikely they would get the business. Following the call he discovered it was going to be equally unlikely to obtain the services of a plane as Heathrow, Gatwick and Stanstead were shrouded in fog. There were no flights into those airports until further notice. The airline anouncement was precise and courteous, but nonetheless infuriating.

With the resignation born of many years of international travel and international frustration, he offered his habitual curse on the gods that had made a sophisticated modern transport system so vulnerable to minute drops of water, looked at his watch, turned on his heel, and decided to go home by an alternative route. He really could not face another night in Brussels. He paused at the airport only long enough to go into the bookshop and try to find something that would suit his disposition. The entire stock of English language books seemed to consist of moronic thrillers or peculiar sex manuals and he decided he was in the mood for neither.

He left the building and took yet another taxi back into Brussels to the railway station. He felt soiled and weary; the lobster was taking revenge on his stomach lining. A faint but definite pain was growing behind his eyes and he was beginning to wish that he, or the world, could stand still for a moment. One compensation was that he had at least missed Celia's dinner party and all the superfluous, polite conversation and over-rich food that was habitual on such an occasion.

Mark Telford was not a man given to fantasies but there, in the middle of Brussels, he yearned for the sight of some green fields and clean air and felt the overwhelming diesel fumes sinking deep into his lungs for the umpteenth time that day.

Once on the train, he settled himself into a seat, shut his eyes and leaned back, resigned to yet more inhuman movement. Perhaps, he thought, the Victorians were right when they said that man was not meant to travel faster than 20 miles an hour. What interest am I paying, he wondered, on my life?

A large man with three suitcases and a brown paper parcel tapped apologetically on Mark's shoulder and pointed out to him that the seat was reserved, a fact which had escaped Mark's preoccupied attention. Mark apologised – he was extremely good at apologies – and taking his bag and suitcase, went into the corridor where he was forced to stand for the best part of the journey.

Peter skated slowly but securely, holding Jenny's hand. The romance which yesterday had been completely finished was now on again. Jenny had firm, fine looks not, he thought to himself drily, unlike his mother's. Perhaps it was true that young men were drawn to younger versions of their mothers. Watching her stand out amongst the expert skaters who wheeled and whirled about them, Peter had lost track of how long they'd been on the ice, and suddenly noticed Jenny had begun to look tired.

She was obviously pleased when Peter gestured to the café area and they slithered over to the fencing, removed their boots and padded off to buy a Coca Cola and find some seats. Before long their conversation turned, as it frequently did, to the question of schools and 'A' levels and careers and what parents expect and what they ought to expect of parents. Peter was still undecided about his university career. Economics had always been a favourite subject and Jenny thought that if Peter were to become an economist it would please his father.

'No, not really. I don't think he particularly wants me to follow him into the Bank,' Peter said slowly.

'That's good,' smiled Jenny. 'Parents who give their sons a stethoscope or document case for their christening present are really boring.'

Peter's expression became serious. 'Dad's not like that,' he said. 'In fact, he's so fed up with banking at the moment he's probably positively against me going into it.'

'I thought he was doing well – travelling all over the place and so on.'

Peter shook his head. 'He's doing well enough, but it's taking up all his time. He hardly manages to get out on the boat at all. It just sits on the Thames rotting away.'

Jenny quickly related this to the woman's point of view. 'Your Mum must get fed up with it too,' she said.

'She does a bit – though she keeps very busy with her committees and things. It's hard to know why they bother . . . you know . . . staying married at all.'

Jenny responded instantly. 'Peter! That's a terrible thing to say! Marriage isn't all sex, and holding hands. It's a partnership, working together . . . all that.'

'Maybe – but that seems to involve seeing one another occasionally.'

Jenny smiled. 'Yes well that does tend to help a relationship!'

Peter slowly met her eyes and realised that if, superficially, she resembled his mother then perhaps she might not be too far wrong in seeing in him just a hint of his father. 'Point taken!' he said.

Some miles away arabesques of a more ethereal nature were taking place in the conversation at Celia's dinner party. Among the ladies of the Theatre Grants Committee these calorific social events were not really an excuse for eating and talking but an equivalent to mountaineering. Each new dinner must be a culinary summit greater than those which had gone before. At Celia's this evening the leg of lamb *Duxelles* had brought forth particular praise for the subtlety of the flavours; and became the subject of a debate as to whether it was the special qualities of the garlic or the arrowroot which gave it its unique flavour. Max, having paid his compliments to the cook, paid even greater implied compliments to Sylvia, though not without teasing her for her speech, in that day's meeting.

'Quite a revolutionary, our Sylvia,' he said.

'I certainly am not,' replied Sylvia, but Max continued, undeterred, 'She kept us in committee all day fighting for the horny-handed miners of some Northern town or other . . . '

Sylvia opened her eyes innocently. 'Perhaps I just like strong men, Max!' she said. Considerable laughter greeted this remark, but Max was not put down. 'Oh I see,' he said, 'it's all clear now! I thought you were fighting for their artistic souls – but it was just a bit of rough trade you were after!'

Celia Hawkins, who was as unshockable as a high-voltage insulator, pretended outrage. 'Max!' she exclaimed. Sylvia was unruffled.

'It's all right, Celia, I think it's probably true. Not sexually of course, but the art scene can get . . . well, a bit pretentious sometimes . . . crazy even . . . ' Despite the pleasant banter, Sylvia was missing Mark. During her every day life she was totally accustomed to his absence, but on social occasions, when, as so frequently happened, he was detained, delayed, or in a meeting, she felt almost incomplete. Max was taking his duties as her partner seriously, and when he suggested that he drive her home, Sylvia had no hesitation in agreeing.

The darkness was thick with fog and the sodium street-lamps were hazy pin-points in the deep murk. It was very quiet in the Mercedes. At twenty miles an hour the engine was almost silent and the only intrusive noise was the flick, flick, flick of the windscreen wipers. Max was quiet too, staring out intently to catch the first hint of an on-coming car.

'My God, I'm glad I'm not driving in this fog. It is good of you Max,' Sylvia said.

Max risked a quick smile in her direction. 'Not at all, it's hardly out of my way. Very sensible of you not driving to the party.' There was a pause before he added '*Where is* Mark tonight?'

'Goodness knows . . . Brussels . . . or on his way home . . . or off somewhere else. He was in Germany this morning and he could be at home now . . . 'Again there was a pause in which the wipers flicked ineffectually at fog.

'It must be difficult for you both,' Max observed gently.

'Neither of us want to live in the other one's pocket,' said Sylvia. 'We both have our own lives and interests and so on, but at present that's *all* we have.'

Max risked another smile in her direction.

Mark stood on the deck of the ferry. All colour was soaked up by the fog and the most tangible thing in his small world was the throb of the engines through the boards under his feet. Uncomfortable though it was, he preferred it to the cloying atmosphere below decks where the passengers were consuming as much of the cheap spirit as they possibly could during the crossing. Mark felt curiously cleansed by the foggy night, though he would have infinitely preferred sailing in more luminous conditions. At least, he was not required to make any decisions during the voyage and for as long as it lasted, he was protected from the telephone, the business minute, the accountants, the clerks, the bosses and the ever-questioning juniors. He looked at his watch, peering closely through the gloom, clutched his coat a little more tightly around himself and walked carefully around the planking. Calm though it was, he found a pretty girl of about eighteen, vomiting quietly into the wash. He muttered a sympathetic word to her, and continued. As soon as the ferry docked at Dover and he had cleared customs and immigration he made for a telephone booth.

As Sylvia stepped from the car she could hear the telephone ringing. 'Do come in Max,' she called as she hurried up the path and fumbled her key into the keyhole. Leaving the door open behind her she switched on the light and picked up the telephone. Mark's voice was quite distinct despite the crackly line.

'Hello darling,' he said.

'Where are you?'

'Would you believe, Dover?'

'Dover! What on earth are you doing there?'

'Fog at London airport.'

Sylvia glanced towards the door. Max was just coming in.

'Yes, it's bad here too,' she said. 'Still there must be plenty of trains.'

There was a pause before he answered. 'No, I'm staying at an hotel.'

'But why?' she demanded. 'It would only take you a couple of hours.'

'Yes I know,' said Mark, 'but I thought while I was actually in Dover I'd stop over to look at a site a client is thinking of buying.'

Sylvia suddenly felt the irritation she had hidden all evening explode and she couldn't help but snap, 'Oh, Mark! So when *will* you be home?'

Mark adopted his customary slight stammer, a sign of his mind working as he spoke. 'Tomorrow sometime. I'll get away from here about mid-day. I have to go into the city but I'll be home after that.'

Now there was an unmistakable shift in Sylvia's voice, from irritation to resigned pleading. 'You will he home for supper won't you? We have Simon and Mary coming round.'

Mark assured her that he would indeed be home for the supper, and asked her how her evening had gone. After her vague assurance that it was pleasant, they said goodnight and rang off. Sylvia had almost forgotten Max's presence but when she turned from the telephone he was standing, the door not quite closed, looking tall and dignified, quietly waiting for her to finish.

'Oh, Max,' she said, 'I'm sorry . . .'

'Mark not coming home?' It seemed more like a statement than a question.

Sylvia sighed. 'No . . . stuck in Dover overnight . . .'

'I'm sorry,' he said. 'Well I must be off.' Sylvia moved to the door and closed it. 'I was just thrown by that phone call,' she said. 'Would you like a drink or a coffee before you go?'

'Coffee sounds good.' He followed her through to the kitchen, and perched himself on a stool. He watched her silently as she poured the beans into the grinder, ground them and tipped them into the Cona.

'Sylvia,' he ventured. 'What are you going to do when you get bored with our little committee?'

She turned to him in surprise. 'What on earth do you mean?' she demanded.

Max shrugged, determined to say his piece. 'I watch you there arguing, debating, suggesting crafty little compromises that the opposition jump at only to discover you've given nothing away what so ever. You could take on the rest of the committee in your sleep and beat them hands down.'

Sylvia turned back to the Cona and carefully twisted the top bowl into the lower. 'Including you?' she asked.

'No, not including me. You see you've done it again, slipped round an awkward question. What are you going to do when you get bored with it?'

Sylvia opened the fridge and took out a carton of cream which she quickly decanted into a jug. 'How can I answer a question like that. For a start how do you know I'm going to get bored?'

'Because you'll get fed up giving advice that's seldom heeded. You'll want some executive position.'

She put the jug and saucer on the table in front of Max and looked him straight in the eye.

'How do you know?' she said, almost banging the cup down in front of him.

'I can't *know*, of course, but I think it's likely,' Max smiled. 'Forgive me my dear,' said Max. 'My interest is purely paternal I assure you. I suppose I just resent seeing so much ability wasted. I've never got out of being a teacher perhaps. Tell me, what would your husband think of your working full-time?'

'I don't know,' said Sylvia. 'We haven't discussed it; it's not easy, is it?'

The front door opened with a familiar bang that announced Peter's arrival home from his skating session with Jenny. He came through to the kitchen.

'Sorry,' he said. 'I didn't know anyone was here.'

He eyed Max speculatively, computing in an instant the

possibility that his mother might find this man who was perhaps twenty years her senior attractive, that perhaps he might have interrupted something more than a friendly cup of coffee.

'Don't be silly darling,' said Sylvia. 'You know Max, don't you?'

Peter crossed to Max and shook his hand. Max, already standing now, looked at his watch, and said that it was time he was going. Sylvia showed him to the door. As she was opening it for him, he said, 'I hope I haven't . . . trespassed.'

'What an odd word to use. I'm certainly not furious with you Max, if that's what you mean.'

They exchanged a smile and Max walked off into the fog and the darkness.

Peter was pouring himself what was left of the coffee from the Cona. 'I'm sorry if I broke that up,' he said, as she came back into the kitchen.

Sylvia sensed at once what was in the back of his mind.

'You didn't break anything up. Don't be silly Peter. There was nothing to break up.'

Peter waved his coffee laconically, with all the wordly wisdom that seventeen years bestows; that generosity of the younger generation towards the older which implies that there is no need for further pretence of perfection, no experience unknown, no foible undeserving of sympathy.

'Well, I don't know do I?' he said. 'I mean with Dad away so much it would be perfectly reasonable for you to have a boy friend, wouldn't it?'

Sylvia sensed at once a point which she could exploit. 'A boy friend would be lovely,' she said, 'but it's rather a long time since Max was a boy, don't you think?'

As she went up to bed Sylvia found herself wondering if Max was right when he suggested that all her word play – her genuine delight in never losing a verbal encounter – was really a substitute for action.

The hotel room was more marked by what it lacked than what it possessed. The hand basin had faint hair cracks around the plug hole, there was no fridge stocked with little bottles of every kind of spirit and cold continental beer, there was a black and white television and a piped radio service. As he cleaned his teeth, and spat the white foam over the little cracks, Mark was struck with a sudden sense of adventure, and equally, as a following thought, he was aware of how ridiculous that feeling was. After travelling Europe for – how many years was it? – it was absurd to consider a commercial hotel in Dover in any way exciting or adventurous. But that mood which he had generated on the ferry, of being cocooned away from the clamour and the dealers and the lunch time conversations and the polite expressions of worry, the delicate probings of bargaining even, had remained with him. He buttoned his pyjamas slowly, stretched and slipped between the sheets, put out the light and fell immediately into a deep sleep.

He woke at eight in the morning, climbed quickly out of bed and drew the curtains. The fog had thinned into a translucent mist. He remembered mornings in his childhood when the family had arrived at a hotel late in the evening, too late to adventure to the shore, and that morning thrill of remembering that one was beside the sea. He found the bathroom, bathed and made his way down for a light breakfast. He bought a copy of the *Financial Times* but barely glanced at the statistical pages, reading instead the news. Outside the hotel the sun had risen clear of the grey Dover buildings and was quickly dispelling the mist. Mark set off towards the sea glancing up at the sea-gulls which circled squawking above him. He made his way down to the promenade where at this early hour there were few other people and leaned against the iron ballustrade. The tide was high, knocking the shingle to and fro with an insistent spitting noise. The sky was full of gulls coming down through the mist, wheeling and falling to the sea as they searched for breakfast.

An early ferry with a plume of smoke over its funnel was surging out into the Channel. Mark felt not the slightest wish that he were on on it, and smiled. He strode out along the promenade until he came to the yacht harbour where the morning activity was well under way, an activity that he immediately understood. There was no twist of rope, no bobbing buoy, no shifting dinghy that did not call to him. He wished fervently that his own boat were riding there and that he had nothing else to do but put stores on board, check the sails and prepare for a long relaxing voyage – a voyage with no business objective, indeed no purpose at all except the enjoyment of being close to the water and the wind.

A ketch was being prepared to sail. A boy of Peter's age stood on the deck and his father called to him, 'Get ashore Jeremy and prepare to cast off!'

Mark stepped forward to the bow walk and called, 'It's all right I'll cast off!' The man looked up and called out his thanks. 'Going far?' Mark asked.

'Boulogne!' the man shouted. 'Last trip of the season.'

'Marvellous! I wish I were going too.' Mark reached down and took hold of the rope. 'Cast-off for'ard!' Mark called, throwing off the warp.

The boy took his long hook and pushed the bow away from the quay, the water surged up and splashed. Mark seized the bow-warp, unwound it and flung it as hard as he could. 'Cast-off stern!' he shouted. The engine revs built and the ketch moved slowly away towards the lock. 'Bon voyage!' Mark shouted out to them. The man called his thanks as they both waved.

Mark stood there for several minutes watching the craft. A pair of gulls flew behind it circling ready in case there should be a promised fish. The air was full of aromas of the sea, and the salty quayside tang of fish. It was pure delight.

Mark forced himself to look at his watch, and decided that business must at last be placated. From where he stood he could see thc town nestled in the arms of the hills and could see through the mist the arching cliff that would forever be a symbol of England. He began the walk back into the grey streets of Dover.

He stopped idly at a couple of shops with no intention of buying anything. They were full of intriguing things that Mark either possessed or could well live without. An old grey-stone building caught his eye. Across the front of it in raised silver letters were the words Knight's Bank. This was surely the right place to start his explorations, his tentative search for a clue that would help him to secure the Manton's loan.

The bank had just opened. He went to one of the two cashiers, and passed over a cheque and his cheque card. He took the money and then asked, 'What's the name of the Manager, please?'

'Mr Stetchley,' the girl replied.

Mark was surprised. '*Tom* Stetchley?' he asked.

She nodded.

'Will you tell him that Mark Telford would appreciate a word with him?'

The girl weeded her way through the neat arrangement of desks, telephones, filing cabinets and computer terminals to the open door of the Manager's office. Only a few seconds passed before the dapper familiar figure of Tom Stetchley, stepped from the office and approached Mark smiling, his arm stretched out ready for a hearty handshake.

'Mark Telford . . . well, well! What on earth are you doing here . . . ?'

Mark grasped his hand. 'I could ask the same,' he said. Tom Stetchley waved him into his office and asked the bank clerk to bring two cups of coffee.

Tom Stetchley had been the Manager of the first branch in which Mark had worked when he joined Knight's, a man whom Mark had both admired and respected for a long time. Tom quickly made it clear that he had been following Mark's rise through the ranks with considerable interest, and was well briefed on all the articles that appeared in the bank's news sheet about him. Mark said that it was really nothing significant, but Tom would have none of that. 'Don't say that,' he said, 'you're one of my few successes in the bank.'

'Tom!'

'When you're Chief General Manager,' Stetchley went on, 'I'll be able to say "He's a good lad is Telford. I started him off you know, he started in the bank the same day I had my first manager's office." '

'That seems a long time ago,' Mark said.

'And I'm still here and you are up in the stratosphere . . . ' said Stetchley, holding out his hand to take the tray of coffee. 'Now what *are* you doing here?' he asked.

Over coffee Mark explained his conversation with

Dupont and how they had little chance of being offered the opportunity to lend Manton's a substantial capital sum. A little exploration, he thought, a little poking about might give Mark just the information that might impress them and perhaps show that a British bank with an office in Dover could give them better service than a bank based in Zurich. After all, banking, as Tom Stetchley well knew, was more than simply giving out and taking in money. 'Of course,' Mark went on, 'now I know his local manager will be Tom Stetchley, it's in the bag!'

'But it won't be,' said Tom Stetchley, shaking his head, 'I'm retiring in a month.'

Mark was puzzled. He frowned. 'Surely not? You can't be at retiring age yet?'

Tom explained that he was going a couple of years early. Not because of health reasons, as Mark had first thought, but because he offered to resign and the bank had not refused him. Mark paused a moment, waiting to hear the real reason behind the early retirement of a manager as good as Tom Stetchley.

Tom looked into his coffee. 'I'm a dinosaur Mark,' he said. 'This job isn't the same as when you walked into the branch all those years ago. I'm not a manager. I'm a bloody salesman! I mean look at this lot!' Stetchley pulled open the drawer of his desk and took out dozens of brochures, for credit cards, for loans, for personal finance, for insurance, for wills, for mortgages . . . 'Look what they want me to sell. Insurance, hire-purchase, factoring stocks and shares, even holidays!'

Mark leaned forward over Stetchley's desk and said, 'Well, we're no longer just a bank but a financial group.'

Tom Stetchley shook his head with exactly the gesture that Mark remembered him using when he had gone to Stetchley with some problem that his old manager had considered absurd. 'I know all that,' said Stetchley, 'and I'm no longer a bank manager but a *groupie* following the trendy ways of lending out money as if it's confetti.'

'Oh Tom, you always were very conservative.'

'Right, and I still am! Do you really think it's a good thing to try to get our customers into debt? I mean, tell me honestly, Mark. Is it a good thing? We give them credit cards, personal loans, cheque guarantee cards, cash cards. We try to get them in hock to us – and the Country in hock to the I.M.F. or any other international bank which is daft enough to lend us . . . it's lunacy. So now you can see why Head Office can bear to part with me.'

Mark leaned back again in his chair and sipped his coffee. He said gently, 'You haven't changed Tom, not one bit. I remember how customers used to say to me on the desk "Is Mr Stetchley in a good mood?" if they wanted an overdraft.'

'I think they still do,' said Stetchley. 'Well, anyway, I hope one of the last useful things I can do in this branch is to give you some assistance. But what was the first thing I taught you about lending propositions?'

Mark smiled. 'Always visit the client on his own patch and have a good look.'

Tom Stetchley nodded. 'Right,' he said.

'But he isn't there. It's just a field,' Mark observed.

Tom Stetchley shook his head, and said, 'You never know what you don't know 'til you you know all there is to know.'

'I could have said it with you,' said Mark and smiled again. 'I must ring Head Office first, they haven't a clue where I am.'

Philip Haslet was by no means convinced that the investment of Mark's time would bring any dividend. Mantons was a blue chip company and could command the lowest rates of interest available. But Haslet agreed that a few hours snooping would not be a grave waste of time.

Ten minutes later, Mark and Tom Stetchley were driving out of Dover. The warmth of the sun had lifted most of the mist, but there was still enough to give the fields a hazy translucence like a temporal landscape. This was for Mark a far more enjoyable ride than his Brussels taxi had afforded. The leaves on some of the trees were showing their first buds and blossoms of early spring.

The proposed site for the Manton factory was set in beautiful rolling countryside. So beautiful, in fact, that Mark began to doubt that they would get planning permission. Tom Stetchley agreed that there would be a great deal of struggle with opposition pressure groups headed by the conservationists. But he was sure, with unemployment as high as it was and Manton's having no factory in England, that planning permission would eventually be granted.

'You know the policy as well as I do,' Tom Stetchley said, as they walked into the long grass of the field. 'But you probably don't hate it as much. We're like a maiden lying on her back and begging to be raped. When a big multi-national wants to use our land and resources and skills to make profits to export to America or Brussels or Tokyo, we treat them as though they're doing us a favour.'

Mark didn't waste his time arguing with Tom Stetchley, whose views on this matter he knew well. He pointed out merely that some multi-nationals based in Britain had factories in rather fine French countryside. Stifling for a moment his sense of beauty, Mark began to assess the site commercially; good road to Dover with an excellent container port and the coal field just a short distance away.

'If they say they'll heat with coal and get the N.U.M. behind them,' said Tom Stetchley, 'what will they have to fear from environmental groups?'

Stetchley bent down and pulled a handful of the wet grass. 'You know,' he went on, 'it's a funny feeling selling land to foreigners so near the white cliffs of Dover. A thousand years of defying anyone to take them and now they can have them for a few miserable Euro dollars.'

Now Mark could not resist the inevitable debate. 'You're wrong Tom,' he said, 'absolutely wrong. I'm sorry to disagree so strongly but you are. Those thousand years of defiance have made a lot of graveyards. Those white cliffs are echoed in tombstones all over the world. If we can find a way to work with other countries, in other countries . . . if we can all be so interdependent that wars are impossible, my God, Tom, its worth sacrificing the piddling ideas of Great Britain or little England, if it comes to that!'

Tom Stetchley grinned broadly and threw the grass over his shoulder. 'That's better Mark,' he said. 'You know you really had me worried. You remember all those arguments we used to have? I haven't had any like that since. I know you're older now but I hoped you hadn't changed that much. I was beginning to wonder how far right I'd have to go to get a rise out of you! My next proposition would have been to build gas chambers for clients who had exceeded their over-draft limit.' Mark laughed and kicked a toadstool. 'Don't get me wrong though, Mark,' added Tom. 'I'm in the Right and I am in favour of conservative traditional banking practice.'

On the way back to town Tom decided to take a perhaps unnecessarily long, but definitely scenic route. Mark looked out of the window and saw an abandoned airfield, with tall grass growing through cracks in the runways and dumped rubble lying on the aprons.

'That's a miserable looking place,' he said.

'It's going to look even worse,' said Tom Stetchley. 'The council are going to build a gipsy site on it. The council own it . . . somehow or other they picked it up after the war, so they've no option really.'

Mark frowned. 'The council own that?' he asked. 'Must be what . . . a hundred or a hundred and twenty acres.'

Tom agreed with his estimate. It was at precisely the same moment that they smiled at each other. 'You see Mark. You never know what you don't know . . . '

They laughed together with a sense of achievement.

Back at the bank Mark had to decide whether to take an early train for London or join Stetchley at the Yacht Club. His decision, he realised as soon as he had made it, was inevitable, and so at twelve-thirty he stood at the yacht club bar amongst the signal flags and the bric-a-brac with the other drinkers, a pint of beer in his hand and not a lobster in sight. 'What on earth am I doing, Tom, rushing about all over the place when I could find a billet for myself in a little town like this and start to live sanely again?' Mark observed.

'You're hooked on excitement Mark,' said Stetchley. 'I saw the light in your eyes when you saw that site.'

Mark put his beer on to the bar. 'But, so did yours! And you make just as many decisions a day as I do, and to the people involved the decisions are just as important. After all, if I manage to lend five million pounds to Monsieur Dupont it will be just a ripple on the sea of Manton's finances, whereas you might make a loan of twenty pounds to the father of a family and save them from desperation.'

'I know,' said Tom Stetchley. 'But you're a few rungs up the ladder. You have to take your place on it. Remember I'm the old die-hard. I *believe* in the ladder. I'm proud of you Mark.'

When the time came for Mark to leave, he felt inexplicably sad and happy at the same time. Sad that Stetchley was right, the banking world had changed and in doing so had made a 'dinosaur' out of a very capable and well-meaning person, but Mark felt happy too, for the day had restored his good humour and given him hope for an idea in the future.

After the peace of the Dover promenade, the clean whisper of his feet on the wet grass, and the relaxed atmosphere of the yacht club, the City seemed a seething, boiling torrent of rushing, shouting, noisy humanity. Mark rushed into the Head Office of Knights Bank with the same need for safety with which the man on the ketch would seek harbour if a storm blew up over the Channel. The entrance hall of Head Office branch was like a Victorian church. Pillars soared to meet a vaulted ceiling and the counters had the massive sturdy quality of vast pulpits. Compared to the chatter of the modernised Dover branch the tones of the customers here were hushed and reverent in comparison to the hubbubs outside. There could be no doubt that here, money was an almost spiritual force, a quiet power at the hub of this vast financial wheel to which Mark was by now so accustomed.

After a relaxed morning, Mark swept into Philip Haslet's office as a messenger of news, if not good at least urgent. Without preliminaries Mark asked to use Philip's phone, spoke to his secretary and asked her to make an immediate appointment with Monsieur Dupont wherever the Frenchman wished. He also asked her to book the flight that would get him there. 'Stress how vital it is,' he said. 'Say I have information of immediate concern to his plans.' He put the phone down.

Haslet handed him a whisky. 'Do you really want to tell me what you're doing? It sounds as if you've already got it all buttoned up,' he said.

Mark calmed himself down. 'I'm sorry to put on such a high-powered act, but it really is necessary. I think we're going to have to see the Chief General Manager . . . do you think your secretary can see if he's available in a half an hour or so?'

Haslet visibly bristled at taking an order, albeit such a polite one, from Mark. 'Of course, Mark. I'll call her just as soon as you've told me what all this is about.'

'Philip,' said Mark, 'if I don't get to Dupont by tomorrow lunch time we'll lose a five to ten million pound business – with a possibility of millions more from one of the world's biggest companies. Don't let's lose that because the Chief General Manager went home five minutes early.'

Haslet shrugged, and called through on his intercom. 'Janet . . . Get on to the Chief General Manager's secretary. See if he can squeeze us in in about half an hour. It's important.' He turned to Mark. 'Now, I would like an explanation.'

'The whole deal from Dupont is ten million. Five million for the site purchase, site preparation, site building. Five million for tooling and stocking. Repayment over seven years with interest only on the first two years.

'It sounds a pretty standard deal, except it's a blue chip company that banks with a competing Euro-consortium . . .'

'Right,' interjected Haslet. 'It would have been very attractive.'

Mark drew breath and continued, 'I'm as sure as eggs that we're just window dressing for the Manton board. To show them that Dupont has tried for a competitive tender. But with a blue chip like Manton's, how can you compete? It's one-over-base rate for all of us and we piddle around with hundreds on commission for cash transfer and the rest. But I think I've come up with a way to really make a dent in the figures. The site they want is in beautiful countryside, the type of place where they'll run into all sorts of trouble. But, the county has a site nearer Dover which is more or less derelict that the government is leaning on them to turn into a gipsy site.

'It means they have to lay on sewers, run water to the site, the whole works . . . more or less for nothing. Now the county has problems with public opinion about siting the gipsies there. But if they could borrow from us, do a real job on it for say a quarter of a million, a short road, sewers, water, then lease a hundred acres to Mantons at say twenty-five thousand pounds a year, which would cover their interest payments to us, on their remaining twenty acres they can put their gipsies – free! All water and so on will be there!' So . . . they get a free gipsy site, public opinion will swallow the gipsies if they get another six hundred jobs, and the rates on the factory are all profit to the authority.'

Mark paused, aware that Haslet was listening intently.

Haslet's normally stolid features were beginning to crack. He was becoming excited. 'And Manton's will get a cheap site *and* save a million or so on site purchase and preparation. Clever! So all you need is the authority from the C.G.M. to lend to the Local Authority, and we're seeing him in a few minutes . . . by the way does the Authority know that it's going to ask us to lend it a quarter of a million?'

'No, not yet,' said Mark. 'The Chief Executive does and he's laying on emergency meetings of the Planning Finance and General Purposes committees.' For ten minutes Mark and Haslet went over the details to make sure they were water-tight. They were interrupted by a buzz from the intercom to tell them that the Chief General Manager could see them.

The Telfords' dining-room was full of warm wood and glistening silver. The table was blessed with flowers and candles. Mary was wearing a very low cut black dress and Sylvia wondered to herself how Mary had kept her breasts so firm. She must be forty-five if she was a day, Sylvia was thinking. Simon, a heavily-built, balding man with lifeless grey eyes and an irritatingly slow way of eating, was expounding to Peter on the virtues of private medicine. Peter was saying very little, concentrating on his food and trying not to say anything too provocative.

Sylvia was acutely aware of the empty chair. Her sense of irritation, which yesterday had been restrained by her acceptance of necessity, was now flexing its muscles. She was talking intelligently enough with Simon but her eyes flicked continually from Mary's abnormally uplifted breasts to the vacant chair. Simon was launching into his third major speech, this time on the the quality of life in relation to the bank balances which people acquired only through skill, industry, intelligence and breeding, when the front door clicked open.

Sylvia excused herself and went through to the hall. Mark looked very tired. The slight shadow around his sharp eyes was darkened by fatigue. It had obviously been a difficult meeting.

'Oh Mark,' she said, 'why are you late? You know they're always early. We're half-way through dinner!'

Mark's manner was hesitant but he was ruled by his tiredness.

'I'm sorry,' he said, 'really sorry, but it was unavoidable.'

'It always is.' Sylvia snapped and then she turned without kissing him and went back into the dining-room. Mark hung up his coat, put down his document case and his suitcase, adjusted his tie and went through to the dining-room in her wake. He made his apologies with a pleasant smile. Mary expressed amazement at the scope and range of his travels, particularly when he pointed out that the following day he would have to be lunching in Paris.

'Oh no!' Sylvia let slip.

'I'm afraid so darling, I've a lunch appointment there.'

'No wonder my bank charges are so high!' Simon commented, smiling around the table in expectation of applause.

Mark was sufficiently tired to be direct. 'No Simon,' he said, 'The cost of the lunch will ultimately be borne by your patients. I'm lunching with the finance director of Manton's, the manufacturing pharmacists.'

Sylvia said nothing, Peter was looking intensely at his food and Mary took it upon herself to divert the subject. She leaned forward, giving Mark an excellent view of her cleavage, smiled and said in an excited girly manner, 'Well it all sounds very exciting and jet-setting!'

'Yes it does doesn't it, but I'll let you into a secret,' said Mark. 'Working lunches are not much fun if you have to work during them – nor are working breakfasts, even if you don't. And finally no lunch, not even in Maxim's of Paris, can survive an aperitif called Heathrow.'

Mark realised he'd been rather blunt and relented by

giving them a quick resumé of the last two days, including his meeting with Stetchley. 'Old Tom was one of your real old gentleman bankers,' he continued. 'The daily balance was only marginally less important than the ten commandments, and he ran his branch like a Guards battalion. The cashiers wouldn't dream of wearing anything but a formal suit. I do believe that the customers felt that they had to put on a tie before cashing a cheque. I'm afraid computerised book-keeping and girl cashiers who look like go-go dancers have finished him. He's retiring early.'

Sylvia asked Mark if he'd like some of the casserole that she had so carefully prepared that afternoon, but he declined, choosing instead some wine and a little cheese. When she protested that that was not much he said that after chasing around all day he really would prefer just to sit and perhaps have something a little later.

Simon moved swiftly into the realm of doctorial pronouncement. 'You ought to eat properly Mark. When you're lying in intensive care fighting a coronary, none of this will seem at all important.'

Mark lifted his glass and Sylvia poured some wine for him. 'I realise that,' he said. 'What worries me more is that recently a coronary seems almost attractive.'

'Mark!' Sylvia exclaimed.

'I don't mean death,' he went on. 'I mean a little gentle stab so you could say to yourself and the world, right that's enough.'

'That's terrible Mark,' Mary exclaimed. 'No job's worth that.'

Instead of answering her Mark pointed out that Simon's role as a consultant frequently involved broken nights, early mornings and irregular meals, and hustling to one point from another without pause for thought. Mary had no choice but to agree.

'There you are then,' said Mark, 'that's what is so attractive about branch banking. At the end of the day you balance the books and no one can present a cheque at thirty two minutes after three anywhere in the country to spoil your balance. Stasis for eighteen hours until 9.30 the next morning.'

'I diagnose a serious case of nostaligitis,' Simon said,

holding his glass up like a measuring instrument. 'The best cure is homoeopathic therapy. It's a system where a disease is treated by minute doses of drugs which cause the same symptoms as the disease. In Mark's case I should think a week as a branch bank manager should effect a complete cure.

One could tell from Simon's manner why it was that consultants were almost universally loathed by nurses.

'Cynic!' said Mark.

The argument then turned to the relative values of medicine, the National Health Service and Banking. To Sylvia it seemed but an extension of the same argument as it had been conducted across candle-lit dinner tables for many years. When Mark said that someone had to provide the money for health services, social security and roads, Simon replied that bankers produced nothing tangible but merely moved cowrie shells, keeping one back out of ten for themselves. When he added that this was an unnecessary and expensive mechanism, and Mark insisted that it was not expensive, Simon invited him to walk around the city of London and then around his local hospital and then see who was spending the money. Mark's nerves were plainly jangled as a result of too many hours already spent that day in intense debate, and he thanked God when the front doorbell rang and Jenny arrived.

The arrival of Peter's girlfriend provided a good opportunity to change the subject on to more trivial and less contentious lines.

Sylvia washed up the dishes in a way that unmistakably betokened the disastrous evening. Mark tried to help her but his mind and his will were not in it. Finally he invited her to get it off her chest and tell him off for spoiling the supper party.

'I'm glad you realise you did,' she said.

'Sylvia, Simon is always niggling at me . . . I don't understand it, he's got a good job, security, nice home; why is he so critical?'

Sylvia slammed a plate into the dish-washer. 'Why are you so sensitive?' she said, with no real query in her voice.

'One would have to be insensitive to the point of morbidity not to feel the barbs of Simon's observations.'

Sylvia turned. She wiped her hands on her apron, paused a moment and then let him have it. 'The problem is, you are always too tired to act as a host in your own home. Having guests is such a bore for you, you can hardly be civil.' Mark made to interrupt but she continued, 'Oh you're fine when you have Philip Haslet to dinner, yes sir, no sir, three bags full sir. *I'm* talking about guests who won't help you to the boardroom.' They stood staring at each other for a long moment. Sylvia's remark was sufficiently true to hurt. Or perhaps it was he who hurt himself by the realisation that there was no defence that would not seem like special pleading.

He turned, walked slowly out of the kitchen into the sitting-room and poured himself a large brandy. He slumped into an armchair and sat hunched over the drink, cradling it in his hands. Before he had felt tired, now exhaustion gripped him completely. He could hardly keep his eyes open. What was the point of it all, he wondered, why did he do it? For whom? What was the exchange between the bank and himself, and Sylvia and Peter and this large house where he spent so little time? Sylvia appeared in the doorway slowly, carefully. She'd taken off her apron. He noticed for the first time how lovely she looked with her hair neatly done and a beautiful russet brown dress on. She paused a moment before speaking and said quietly, 'I'm sorry. That was an appalling thing to say.'

Mark looked up at her and then dropped his head again to the brandy with a brief nod.

'I'm sorry,' she said again.

'Let's forget it shall we?' said Mark finally.

But this was a further irritation to Sylvia who did not want to forget it but wanted to resolve it. What was the point, after all, in her saying anything, even too much, if it was simply forgotten, unregistered, unremarked. She took a step into the room. 'Is that all you're going to say?' she said with quiet determination. There was more than a hint of accusation in her voice.

Mark raised his head again. He spoke tersely, through the tiredness, the weariness, that would allow him no more strength for the problems of the day. 'What else is there to say? You've said you're sorry. I've said we'll forget it.'

Sylvia stood for many seconds staring at him. She was struck again with the fact that the last few days seemed to have added years to his appearance. It was a disturbing moment. She could see in his face, the broad temples, the fair hair now tinged with grey, a shadow of all the things she loved and valued and remembered about Mark. Perhaps it was his business-like qualities that appealed to her Scots canniness. And Mark had charm, there was no doubt of that. She longed for them to break through the barrier that had come between them. Like the previous days' fog it seemed to have crept up on them silently, but was now making any communication difficult. Perhaps after all Mark was right to avoid embarking on a long, potentially bitter, but certainly difficult examination of their relationship at this late hour. His tiredness, her irritation and the wine and spirits they had consumed might well allow too much to be said and then perhaps not forgotten.

'Goodnight,' she said, and quickly left the room. Mark looked after her at the empty doorway and listened to the soft sound of her feet on the stairs. He looked towards the piano and wondered whether Chopin would take a little of the day from him. But he realised that he was too tired even for that. He raised the brandy glass and felt that the fumes in his nostrils were as much of a purging as he could expect.

The next morning the sky was clear and blue. At ten thirty Mark was only twenty-five thousand feet from Dover again but this time the distance was vertical not horizontal. He wished that he might bridge that twenty-five thousand feet and be standing again with Tom Stetchley in the green field with the dew. But he turned back to his newspaper and his documents and prepared himself to meet Dupont.

Dupont was late for the meeting, apologetic, complaining that bankers were too hospitable and too generous with the aperitifs. Perhaps, because of his late arrival he got quickly to business, pausing only to order gin and tonics from the waitress. There was a little coaxing between them, a little more of the flashing of verbal foils before Mark commented on how strong the environmental lobby was getting in France.

'Indeed,' said Mr Dupont, 'they are a real force.'

Mark said that, in England too, the environmental lobby was becoming powerful, although things were done differently. Endless enquiries, long delays, such as the nuclear enquiry at Windscale. While the French sent in the riot police to knock protest on the head, in England things were done much more slowly. In England, Mark pointed out, there were no riot police worth mentioning and Manton's chosen site was after all very beautiful.

'You've seen it?' Dupont asked incredulously.

Mark affected the pose of a man cut to the quick. 'Well, of course, Monsieur. We take your enquiry seriously.'

Dupont said he was impressed and plainly he was.

'I can foresee difficulty in planning permission,' Mark went on, 'You will win in the end of course, but you may think that to take on the environmentalist lobby and beat them and go on to build a huge factory in a beautiful and sensitive part of England is not perhaps the best way to introduce yourself to English public opinion, and there's also the cost factor – very high for such beautiful land.' Mark ignored the gin and tonic that the waitress placed by his elbow. He smiled, leaned back in his chair and said, as though he had just found a five pound note, 'It happens I know of a site near Dover. About a hundred acres would be available to you – completely prepared for building. An access road, water and main sewerage. I think you could lease this land for say twenty-five thousand pounds a year – and you would need to borrow a million less.'

Dupont clutched his drink as though it was the most important thing in the world. He looked over the rim of the glass and said, 'Planning permission?'

Mark knew that the hook, if not bitten, was at least inside his adversary's mouth. Now he leaned forward, and tapped his table with his long fore-finger, and said, not too forcefully, 'Ah well, that's the beauty of this scheme. You see it's owned by the local authority and they have their own reasons for wanting to develop. You will appear like knights in shining armour to rescue a derelict site.'

Dupont put his glass down carefully on the table; he leaned forward. 'And you can deliver this?' he asked very seriously.

Mark picked up the menu and glanced over its expensive list of oh-so-perfect food. 'Well,' he went on, 'it's all subject to negotiation of course, but my bankers are at this moment working with the Authority and with our good offices I think that there should not be too much difficulty.'

'How long?' Dupont asked.

Mark waited a moment longer before replying, speculatively, 'A month?'

Dupont's drink was still untouched. 'And your interest rate on ten, no nine million?'

Mark came straight back at him. 'Our best of course. One over base rate . . . '

Dupont continued with the questions. 'Servicing? you have a local branch for cash transmission and so on?'

'Oh yes. Fully adequate and we shall be conscious of the need to offer the best commission rates.'

Dupont needed a moment to think about this. He took his menu, and, after long consideration selected a light, but appetising meal. The waitress stood attentively and took the order. Dupont sipped his gin and tonic.

'What's your local man like? It must be quite a small branch?'

'He's retiring,' said Mark. 'Good thing really. It will enable us to put in a top man, fully capable of servicing your very large business.'

Dupont waved around the attractive dining-room. He looked at Mark for a moment before saying, 'Monsieur, I think I should like this lunch to be on Manton's.'

The sun was low over the white cliffs, plunging them into grey shadow as Mark walked off the ferry and along the sea front. He spotted a taxi, flagged it and climbed in. He asked to be taken to the castle. He stood in the evening breeze with the golden light falling behind the hills looking down into Dover. The surf was still catching the last of the sun, gleaming orange and white as the breakers fell on to the shingle. The town was small, straggling up into the valley. Not in itself attractive but undoubtedly well sited.

The taxi took him back to the harbour and he sat there on a bollard waiting for the light to go, as the last boats came in for the shelter of the night. The tension went from him with a sudden release. It was as though all the separate parts of his being which had been neatly filed away from each other for days, possibly years, fused in one perfect moment. He felt as though he were a vital conductor between the deepening purple of the sky and grey-green water lapping and thrusting against the stone of the jetty.

A grin spread across his face.

He was still grinning the next morning when he went into the General Manager's office with Philip. Harvey, like Mark and like Philip, had come up through the Bank, and he knew when congratulations were in order.

'First class job, Mark,' Harvey said. 'First class, pulled it right out from under the opposition. I really look forward to the next meeting of the Clearing Banks Committee. Old Feltham will *not* enjoy this, though of course I shan't say anything to him.' He smiled conspiratorily at the others. 'So what's next then for our international whizz kid here?'

Before Philip could speak Mark said, 'There are still some things to tie up on the Manton's deal. I promised Dupont that we would put a top man in at the Dover branch to handle his business. The present manager, Tom Stetchley, is retiring.'

Harvey nodded, 'That's right,' he said. 'Well, we'll just have to find a good man. Not easy mind you . . . but we'll work something out.'

Mark's tone when he spoke was hesitant but thoughtful. 'Actually I do have a suggestion.'

Harvey waited for him to go on.

'Myself.'

The men looked at Mark incredulously. 'You?' Harvey demanded.

'I should like to manage the Dover branch.' Mark said.

Harvey was trying to decide whether he had become the

victim of a practical joke, but the expression on Mark's face convinced him that he should at least argue the point.

'But why? It will be such a step down, such a drop in salary and status. The Bank just couldn't consider it. It has too much invested in you.'

Mark remained very serious. 'Then the Bank had better start considering it or face losing its investment completely.'

This was now a long way past a joke for Harvey. 'You'd leave Knights'?' He demanded.

'Yes,' said Mark quietly. The room had become very silent.

Harvey had not become Chief General Manager without realising that behind almost anyone's large, unexpected gesture there lay a simple, basic dissatisfaction with an aspect of their position. He gestured to a chair, 'Sit down, Mark. Now, tell me, what's behind all this? Trouble at home? Anything we can do?'

Mark waited before speaking. 'There's no dramatic trouble, my wife gets fed up with my absences, but that's just par for the course in the International Division. No . . . it's me. I've decided that my life is absurd. I'm tired of rushing about never knowing where I'm going to eat the next meal – even which bed I'm going to sleep in. I like the sea, I like the country. I don't *have* to lead the life I do, and quite simply, I'm not going to go on leading it any longer.'

Harvey slipped easily into that particular gear of tone which expresses both impatience and concern simultaneously. 'Every one of us has felt like this at some time in our career,' Harvey said. 'Every time I go up to Wales for a spot of fishing, I look at our branch tucked away at the side of the river at Machynlleth. Damn it all, the salmon practically jump into the tills! And I think to myself, now wouldn't it be splendid to run that branch, forget all about Head Office, but I know that after a couple of weeks I'd be screaming to get out . . . dying of boredom. You *can't* go back!'

Mark continued in the same quiet, assured vain. 'Maybe *you* can't, but I can.'

Harvey leant back in his chair, irritated that Mark would

not see sense. He tried another mode of attack 'What does Sylvia think about this?'

'I haven't told her yet. I don't know what she'll think.'

Sylvia thought, quite simply, that Mark had gone crazy. That evening as they stood in the kitchen she was completely bewildered. She had become used to Mark's long absences, accustomed to never knowing where he'd be the next day, or when or not he'd be coming home. But this was a new Mark, quiet, sober, with force and an apparent conviction that was manifestly ridiculous.

'But *Dover*, for Gods sake!' she shouted. 'We'll spend the rest of our lives planning whether we go out and play bingo or stay in and watch tele!'

'You exaggerate, Sylvia.'

'Do I? And what about Peter's school?'

Mark toyed with a salt cellar. 'Obviously this won't be sorted out for a month or two,' he said. 'By the time we actually come to move he'll only have a few months to go.'

'But what months Mark?' Sylvia insisted. "A" levels, his whole future; I absolutely refuse to leave London until Peter leaves school!' This was Sylvia at her most forceful. The hint of Scotland in her accent was becoming stronger with every word, but Mark was not to be deterred.

'Then I shall get a flat and you can come down at weekends – and of course I can come up to town very easily.'

Sylvia sat down, not knowing whether to laugh or to cry. She spread her hands wide. 'And all this,' she said, 'is to cut down on travelling?'

Tom Stetchley was no less surprised, and no less indignant when Mark marched into his office in the Dover branch and announced that he was claiming the right of succession to that neatly polished chair.

'They won't let you, you know,' Stetchley had said. 'You're breaking all the rules. In the pontoon of business you either stick, win or bust.'

But when he walked out of the bank door to be greeted by the sounds and smell of the sea, and the endlessly hovering gulls. Mark knew he had made the right decision, and that he would bring all his formidable powers of bargaining and assertion to secure for himself the Managership of the Dover branch. He leaned on the balustrade of the promenade, watching the white horses galloping in at the turn of low tide, and knew that he really had no choice but to follow his conviction through. For him there could be no more desperate, over-heated, over-excited dashing from capital to capital. He would work here in Dover, but also he would live here.

Chapter Two

Mark used the first forty-five minutes of his journey to catch up on the morning's financial business. But by the time the train neared Folkestone and began its journey round the cliffs, so close to the sea that he felt he could reach out and touch it, Mark found time to sit back and think over the events of the last few days. His abdication from life in the International Division for the sake of peace, had hardly been peaceful. There had been all the problems of finding a cottage with a sensible lease, at a sensible rent. There had been the last desperate efforts of senior management to prevent his going just in case it had been a spur of the moment whim, that he might be too embarrassed to rescind for fear of losing face. And most of all, there had been Sylvia.

He found himself still surprised at her reaction. Perhaps he had been naïve in thinking that she would jump for joy at his rearrangement of their lives, but never in a million years had he expected that awful period of cold discussion. Coldly, logically she had told him that though she was forced to accept his decision, she couldn't like it, she couldn't feel happy with it; it might be a lovely cottage, and he might be indeed have been lucky to have obtained it, but she wanted him to be perfectly clear that, at least until Peter finished his 'A' levels, she would continue her life in London. She accused him – and he saw now that she did so with some justice – of always having made decisions entirely for himself. *He* had decided to go into the International Division without consulting her. *He* had decided to go to Dover without consulting her. He might pretend that his reason for leaving the International Division so suddenly was his concern for their lives. But she wanted him to understand that that was not so, he had changed because he was fed up with her complaints. He was not to delude himself into thinking that he had taken anyone's interest into account but his own. And he was forced to agree that it was tactless and selfish, to make the decision and announce it without consulting her. If he had discussed it with her first and they had agreed, then it would have been their decision. But as it was she had been rail-roaded into a new situation as swiftly and with as much regard as he would have rearranged the clerical duties of a junior clerk.

And then there had been Peter, who, when he had found his father on his own, had first accused him of making unnecessary ripples in their domesticity. But then his youthful worship of the individual's freedom took over and he was forced to give Mark's actions his blessing.

'It's how everyone ought to live,' he said. 'Make up your own mind about what's best for you, then other people can fit in or not as they please. The only silly thing is to have the guilty feelings.'

Mark had been disturbed by this remark. Peter certainly was becoming very perceptive.

The train drew into Dover and interrupted his thoughts. Tom Stetchley was waiting at the station to meet him. He brushed aside Mark's thanks for the kind gesture by saying that he had an ulterior motive – that he wanted Mark to meet one of the Bank's biggest customers, and the only opportunity was in a few minutes time. The man was called Maddox – the Managing Director of Maddox Engineering, a family firm employing about four hundred people on foundry work. Mr Maddox had a very sound account. His overdraft facility was for a hundred and fifty thousand pounds, but mostly it was only running at seventy-five thousand.

'I wish he would borrow more,' said Stetchley. 'He needs

to, but he won't see it. Family firm, safe from take overs, but getting more and more inefficient, I'd say. He needs to re-equip, go after some new business, diversify a bit. But he says he's happy enough as it is.'

Mark pulled a wry face. 'Well, I'm in a weak position to try to convince people that they ought to be high flyers,' he said.

Tom Stetchley jabbed a finger at him. 'You won't be here long.'

Mark laughed. 'I haven't even arrived at the branch yet and you're moving me on,' he said.

Tom Stetchley proclaimed his view that Head Office had some peculiar master plan up their sleeve in allowing Mark to manage the Dover Branch. Banks were not, he suggested, philanthropical organisations, and there must be some other reason for them letting him do it than simply following his suggestion that he would like to.

'What else should I know about Maddox?' Mark asked, diverting the conversation. Stetchley couldn't reply for a moment because he was preoccupied with a French driver who was attempting to drive on the right-hand side of the High Street, amidst much to do and uncharacteristic excitability on behalf of the English population.

'Nothing much,' he went on, when he had negotiated his car around the Citroen CX. 'You'll see him at the golf club from time to time. He's been a leading light in the Chamber of Commerce. Has a couple of sons and a daughter. The boys are studying engineering somewhere. One of them at Oxford I think. The main thing is to try and get him to broaden the base of his firm. The town needs the jobs and the country needs the exports if it comes to that.'

The car drew in through the foundry gates. The smells of hot metal and the clanging ring of hammers and stamping presses followed them through the main door and into the office block. Maddox's office furniture was as solid as he was and a good deal older than his sixty years. He was a direct man, showed them briskly to seats and bade them good morning. He said immediately that he was pleased to meet Mr Telford and if he looked after him as much as Tom Stetchley had done he would have no complaints. He looked Mark up and down. 'Has he told you to nag me into expansion?' he demanded, tossing his head towards Stetchley.

'Oh no, I wouldn't do that. He did mention that you did have the capacity and skill to grow faster than you have done.'

Maddox laughed and turned to Tom. 'Well he's certainly more diplomatic than you.'

Stetchley smiled back at him. 'But he hasn't seen how obstinate you can be.'

Maddox roared with laughter and leaned back in his chair. Then he leaned forward again and tapped his paperweight. 'You see? You see?' he said loudly. 'Some people are very hard to please – I do him the favour of borrowing a paltry seventy-five thousand from him on securities worth a quarter of a million, and he insults me.'

'I know lots of people who would love to be insulted by the offer of a quarter of a million loan,' said Mark.

'But the price,' said Maddox. 'I get through a fair day's work but when I leave it I don't have to worry, but if I got greedy and wanted to be the biggest whatever, wherever, I'd soon be the richest man in the graveyard.'

Tom Stetchley turned to Mark and said firmly, 'You have a hard case here Mark, I'm telling you. Assets completely unused.'

Mark directed his attention back to Maddox. 'And you're not worried about a take-over? You are a public company aren't you?'

Maddox brushed this suggestion aside with a great deal of contempt. 'The family are majority shareholders,' he said. 'We're safe from the pirates. These fly boys who leave themselves no margin, no fat, have no stamina. Well, Maddox's has got some fat and as far as I'm concerned it will stay there to protect us from the cold winds that blow every now and again.'

'Well, it's no part of our business to encourage you to be imprudent, Mr Maddox,' said Mark. 'But you know where we are and you know we'd like to help – if and when you want any help.'

* * *

'That's Maddox,' said Tom Stetchley as they walked up the street to the Bank. 'An interesting man and a personal friend of mine.'

Mark looked shrewdly at his old manager. 'Yes, I could see that,' he said. 'And a part of you thinks it's right to keep so much fat on his firm.'

'I wouldn't say that. No, he does have some assets like some property in the town that's completely unused, but I do understand him. He's comfortable, contented. Why should he suddenly become all London business school and projected cash flow orientated? I've been trying to get him to steer a middle way, but with no luck so far – over to you,' Stetchley went on, as they paused on the bank step. 'Now about Everly, he's the Assistant Manager. I ought to tell you about him.'

'That sounds ominous; what's the matter, can't he add up?' Mark asked.

'No, no, far from it. He's first class, he'll go a long way. He's hungry. Just watch that he lets you manage the branch, that's all. If you don't watch it he'll be seeing all the big customers and allowing you to advance fifty quid to a fishmonger to buy a new slab.'

'I'll watch him,' said Mark, and meant it.

'He's good mind, don't tread on him too hard. The Bank needs high flyers – even if they do crash to earth half-way through.'

Then Stetchley stepped forward again and led them into the Bank. As he expected, all the staff found time to say good morning and look Mark over carefully, trying to decide what kind of a boss he would make. As he walked through to Tom Stetchley's office Mark was trying hard to project those qualities of fairness, firmness, intelligence, consideration, decisiveness that he felt he ought to have. Stetchley called Keith Everly into the office and introduced him to Mark. Keith had a broad face, with perhaps a deceptively innocent look. But if Tom Stetchley said he was clever then Mark was in no doubt that that was a good assessment. He liked Keith's neatly cut hair and smart appearance and then found himself surprised that he should be making such a managerial type of judgement so quickly.

'I've been telling Mr Telford that you're first class and

will steal the bank out from under him if he gives you half a chance,' Tom Stetchley said to Keith.

'That's kind of you, 'Keith said, looking at Mark, not at Tom. Stetchley asked Keith if anything important had happened that morning.

'Well,' said Keith, 'it depends on what you mean by important. We have had a visit from Hetherington, the farmer.'

Tom Stetchley looked puzzled. 'He's not one of ours,' he said.

'No, not yet,' said Everly. 'He's across the way.'

The puzzled expression cleared from Tom Stetchley's face. 'Jackson's got sticky again.' He turned to Mark to give him a word of explanation. 'Jackson's the manager over the way. He's been here about a year. Nice chap. You'll like him. This'll be – what? – the tenth account we've pinched off them?'

'I shall like him very much,' said Mark. 'So what did this chap Hetherington want?'

Keith explained that Hetherington farmed four hundred acres, mostly arable with a bit of fruit, and he now wanted to turn a five acre field into a mixed chalet and caravan complex, a holiday development – Hetherington didn't anticipate any difficulty with planning permission because the field was behind a sheltered belt of trees that his father had planted, and was consequently invisible from the road. He wanted to borrow forty-five thousand pounds for a service track, sanitation and eight chalets, against the security of a hundred acres that were his own, two hundred and fifty on agricultural tenancy and fifty on an annual tenancy.

'Any mortgages on the land?' Mark asked.

'I didn't ask him that. I knew Mr Stetchley would want to see him. I've made an appointment for him at ten tomorrow. There wasn't anything in the diary.'

Tom Stetchley turned back to Mark. 'You see Mark, he's very clever, our Assistant Manager. He always leaves me one question I can ask so I don't feel a complete rubber stamp.'

Keith was not to be out-done by this. 'And he usually finds another dozen I haven't thought of,' he said, and asked if they needed him any longer.

'No,' said Tom. 'You stand out there with your butterfly net and catch more of Jackson's customers that poke their noses round the door.'

Keith Everly went out with a smile and shut the door behind him.

Mark nodded his approval. 'You're very good Tom. I remember when I signed my first customer – a student who opened his account with four pounds. You sent for me and made me feel like I'd just signed up the Shah of Persia.'

Tom took Mark on a tour of the branch to meet the staff, beginning with the Manager's Clerk, Carol Milton. Tom did not need to point out to Mark that Carol was very pretty. But he did tell him that she was sitting her Final Exams in Banking in the autumn. Tom Stetchley insisted on lecturing all the girls in the bank about the need to take their exams. Too many of them left to get married, but Carol, he said, was an exception. Mark thought that he would get on well with Carol. She seemed intelligent and was not an unattractive girl. There followed a stream of pleasant, friendly faces, all of whom only deepened Mark's conviction that he would be happy here.

Carol might have been surprised, together with many of her colleagues, if she could have heard the conversation taking place between Harvey and Haslet safely out of earshot in the Head Office. They were discussing a long range strategy which would mean far fewer branches, far fewer managers and far fewer Carols – looking ahead to the day when almost all transactions would be via credit and cash cards with computer facilities taking the place of many of the human beings who now added and subtracted in small towns all over the country.

Sylvia, too, had been doing some thinking about her life and perhaps the very insecurity of the changes that Mark had forced on her were bringing to a head decisions that she had deferred for too long. She had decided that her social and family reasons for staying in London might be given extra strength if she found an executive position. Max, having assured himself that she had thought it through, was gently encouraging without seeming to push, but he did probe the important question of how her taking a job would affect the marriage. Would it damage it?

'Perhaps I'm frightened of discovering that there isn't much to damage,' she had replied.

Despite the certainty of her decision when she had told Max she was more speculative when she raised the subject with Peter.

'What would you think if I got a job?' she asked.

Peter raised his head slightly before replying and looked for a moment remarkably like Mark. 'Depends on the job, I suppose. I wouldn't be very thrilled if you became a ladies lavatory attendant.'

'I'm serious Peter,' Sylvia said.

'So am I. It would depend on the job . . . but you're on all those committees already. It wouldn't make much difference to me would it? I shall be away soon. What does Dad say about it?'

'I haven't discussed it with him. I'm just trying out the idea on you.'

'Are you trying to find a reason for staying in London?' he asked quietly.

'I don't think so,' she said. 'You'll be going to University. Your father seems to be settling down in a steady job. He'll no doubt be sailing at the weekends or playing golf. I just don't feel ready to . . . vegetate, I suppose.'

'But you still could be trying to find a reason for staying in London,' Peter insisted. He got up from the table and rinsed his coffee cup. 'Will you be talking it over with Dad this weekend?'

'Yes.'

'Would you rather I didn't come?' Sylvia looked at him in surprise. 'Good Lord no!' she said.

Peter started to look uncomfortable. 'Well . . . actually I'd rather come down on Saturday morning if it's all right with you. We're having a group practice tomorrow and I wondered if we could come here, I mean we wouldn't be disturbing anyone, would we?'

Sylvia thought about it for a moment and said slowly, 'I see . . . while the cat's away . . . '

Peter smiled, 'The mice can play rock'n roll. Harmless enough . . . '

The next day was Tom Stetchley's last day as manager of the Dover branch of Knight's Bank. Far from turning his mind away from his duties, he had been thinking hard about the loan application from the farmer, Hetherington.

'It's strange,' he told Mark as they tidied the papers in the office. 'Farmers usually hate campers. I thought it would be a good thing to see him on his patch, find out how he really feels. I don't want you getting into lazy ways. We'll drive out there. All right?'

It was a fine day and once again Mark enjoyed the car ride out into the countryside. They had to reverse a couple of times – not Tom Stetchley's strong point – before they found the track that led to the farm. Mark was trying to form a quick impression of the undertaking. A lot of the grass was very long beside the farm track, and the farm buildings had a broken down, sad air about them. The blue paint on the doors and windows of the farmhouse was cracked and peeling, and farm machinery was rusting in the yard. The garden was untidy and overgrown with weeds. When Mark pointed this out to Tom, he shrugged it off.

'If they can't plough it, nature can have it back. That's farmers for you,' he said.

Hetherington came out of the farm door and walked towards the car to meet them. He was a stocky man with greying hair and weather-roughened cheeks. He walked slowly. It seemed at first sight as though everything was rather too much effort for him. He gave them a quick tour of the farm. There was very little production in the fields compared to the next farm, where the wheat had already been planted in abundance. Hetherington's fields were sad and scrappy, he blamed this on bad weather the previous year which, he said, had prevented him from getting on the land. But Tom whispered to Mark that it had been one of the best autumns for many years.

They passed a small empty cow shed with the byres hanging loose and old straw littered on the floor. There was not a cow in sight. Hetherington agreed that there

4

were no beasts on the farm. They had only kept a couple of cows for the house and fattened a few calves, he said, but they were a lot of trouble just to save a few shillings a week on milk. It wasn't worth it.

Mark was depressed by his trip around the farm. Everything betokened lack of care, decay and lethargy. The farm kitchen was no different. It was very untidy, with heaps of dirty clothes scattered around, mud on the floor, and unwashed pots in the sink. Hetherington laboured for a moment or two to make some space for the men to sit down. Neither of them could disguise their distaste at the environment.

Hetherington put the kettle on to make them a cup of tea. Mark began to ask questions. 'You live here on your own then Mr Hetherington?'

'Yes I do. But what's my personal life got to do with asking for a loan?'

Mark mumbled something placatory and said it was just a question of getting to know the customers in order to know if the Bank could really help. For example, Mark pointed out, the Bank had a really fine agricultural division, with experts.

Hetherington dismissed this. He said one of the reasons he was fed up with Mr Jackson at his own branch was that he was always on to him with suggestions to do this or do that. Mark glanced at Tom Stetchley, who was wearing his most inscrutable expression.

'Tell us about this scheme of yours, then,' Tom Stetchley said, breaking his silence.

Hetherington outlined the scheme, pointing out to them a field hidden by trees, where he wanted to set up his holiday place. He was sure it would work. 'It would need to be really kept up . . . made attractive,' said Tom.

Hetherington turned with the tea pot in his hands and gestured around the shambles in which they were sitting. 'Not like the farm you mean.'

Tom Stetchley shrugged. Hetherington went on, 'It's falling to bits, I know. But we're not talking about the farm, are we?'

'No,' said Mark, 'but we want to be sure that your heart's really in the new project. We haven't studied the figures; however, on the face of it it seems a good idea. But only if you really want it to work.'

Hetherington was silent, while he poured the boiling water on to the tea leaves and rinsed some cups. He laid out the cups and the teapot in front of them and then said to Mark, 'You married?'

Mark ran through the details of the family. Hetherington told him that he had a son and two daughters but that they were not interested in the farm. He also had a wife, he said, but she'd upped and left last year taking the girls with her. The son had gone a couple of years before. He was working in an office in London somewhere. Hetherington tapped the teapot. 'I built this place up. My father left me 20 acres. I've bought another 80 and rented a couple of hundred more. All for our Neil, I thought. Something to hand on to him, you know, like my old Dad did to me. But he weren't interested.'

'And you lost interest in the farm,' Mark commented gently.

Hetherington wouldn't agree to that. 'No,' he said, 'I had a wife, didn't I? And a couple of girls. One of 'em, Joaney, she was very interested. She was only eight but she had a real feeling for it – especially the birds – we used to rear turkeys then as well. Then along came this machinery salesman. Sounds like a joke you hear in the pub, don't it? Did you hear about the commercial traveller going to this farm? Well it weren't no joke. I never thought it would happen to me. Never went anywhere, did we? Happy here. Least, I thought she was. All over in a couple of weeks. A couple of weeks. After 18 years it didn't seem possible. It still don't seem possible . . . '

Mark reached for the teapot and poured tea for Tom Stetchley and himself. 'And now you've decided to make a completely fresh start,' he said.

Hetherington agreed. At least he would see some folk around the place and it would not seem so dead.

'It sounds a good idea . . . Mark said.

'So it will be all right, then? You'll lend me the money?' Hetherington asked.

But Mark was not going to be rail-roaded that easily into a decision. He suggested some alternatives; for example selling the farm. Mark pointed out that from this, Hetherington could probably expect to raise about £100,000. Mark looked across at Tom Stetchley, who nodded his agreement at the estimate.

'You could build your holiday site and have enough left over to live on the income from it – apart from the income from the site.'

Hetherington looked very worried at the suggestion. 'But I couldn't sell the farm,' he said.

'Why not?'

There was a long pause and then Hetherington said, with no trace of the belligerent tone that he had been adopting, but rather more of a human appeal, man to man, 'She might want to come back some day.'

In the car, Tom and Mark could not agree about which policy was preferable.

'There's no real risk in the loan is there? With all that security?' Tom said.

'No, but it's a daft decision. He should either sell the farm or really work it. It's just losing value all the time,' Mark insisted.

Tom drove off the rough, grass-bordered track, and back on to the main road. 'No doubt that's what Jackson's been telling him, and why we've got him. And the chance to lend £65,000 on good security, don't forget.'

'Yes, but it goes against the grain, doesn't it Tom? We're not pawnbrokers, after all, just lending on security.'

Tom drew the car to a halt beside the road, thought a moment and said, 'Oh it's not as bad as that. After all he may be right. His wife may want to come back and want to farm again.'

'One look at that farmhouse and she'd be off again even without a machinery salesman,' Mark added remembering how impossible it was to hurry Tom Stetchley into committing himself before he had had the opportunity for a careful examination of the issues. Then Tom went on gently, 'You could be completely wrong about that. One look at the farm and she could be swept away by remorse and maternal feelings. I mean a chap like Hetherington who could build up a farm like that in the time he had is no fool, or sluggard. He could cope with that house if he wanted to. It's just a plea for help.'

Mark nodded his agreement. 'Of course it is, but what sort of help? Do we enable him to distract himself with another occupation whilst his "plea" is extended to the whole farm and messages are sent by thistle seed all over Kent?'

Tom engaged first gear again and revved the engine gently, taking the car back on to the road. 'It's your decision,' he said. 'My advice is to lend him the money, give him a fresh start, and get him back into the world. I've got a feeling he's too good a man to let 300 acres go to wrack and ruin.'

And that was the end of the discussion. They moved down into the outskirts of Dover and back to the Bank, so that Mark could come to grips with the filing system.

The cottage was long and low, set in a well-kept garden three miles outside Dover. The drive was neatly swept, and inside, it all seemed small and unreal to Mark as he prepared the dinner. He had laid the table for two and uncorked a bottle of good claret to breathe. He went back into the kitchen, opened the oven and checked the leg of lamb which he had pricked and embedded with garlic. The smell was delicious. He heard a car coming up the drive. He wiped his hands on a towel, smoothed his hair down without thinking about it, and went outside.

Sylvia was just stepping out of the car. He kissed her on the cheek and took her suitcase from the boot. She stood for a moment in the doorway looking into the candlelit room.

'Oh Mark, it's lovely! I didn't remember it looked so . . . comfortable.' She stepped inside and Mark followed with the suitcase.

'It was a horrid afternoon when we found it, remember. Pouring with rain.'

'It's wonderful. I feel you ought to carry me over the threshold or something.'

Mark laughed. 'After my first days at the Bank I feel you ought to carry me.'

Sylvia joined in his laughter and then took her case and went up the narrow cottage stairs to prepare herself for the evening. Mark went to the table, lifted the bottle, poured a little of the claret, sniffed the bouquet, sipped it, nodded to an invisible jury the confirmation of his good taste, and went through to the kitchen to carve the lamb. He strained the vegetables, put the sauce into a jug and carried it all through. He called up to Sylvia that it was ready.

She came down the stairs wearing a beautiful kaftan.

'You look lovely,' he said.

She smiled her acceptance of the compliment and came down to the meal.

'This looks delicious,' she said.

'I'm afraid there's only one course with some fruit afterwards, so dive into the vegetables,' Mark told her as he took his glass in his hand and raised it in a toast. 'To Dover.'

Sylvia lifted her glass and joined him, but without joining in the sentiments.

As they ate the food he told her some of the details of his day.

'Did you foreclose on any widows or bankrupt any small shopkeepers?' Sylvia asked, with eyes wide.

'Good Lord, no,' said Mark, 'whatever do you mean?'

'You are always saying that everyone's image of the bank manager is wrong. Well you should start on your son. That's his scenario for your opening scenes.' That was the first reference to Peter, and Mark asked if he was all right. Sylvia said that he was fine. He was looking forward to this evening, which he had said was going to be a 'real knockout!'

Mark grimaced his displeasure at the prospect of an evening of funky music. The meal passed pleasantly, without argument, or any hint of labour or difficulty between them, as Sylvia explained her day and her Theatre Grants Committee meeting. Her only quibble was over the traffic on the A2, which had not pleased her at all.

'It's a pity this place isn't up for sale,' Mark observed.

Sylvia put her knife and fork down. 'Oh Mark,' she said, 'it would be impossible. There's only two bedrooms for a start. I mean, it's charming for a dinner à deux but imagine having a dinner party here.'

'I suppose so,' said Mark sadly.

She looked at him carefully and smiled. 'You have a romantic streak running through you like a stick of rock.'

'Is that so bad?' Mark demanded.

'No. It's the nicest part of you.'

After a pause Mark asked, 'How's that chap who runs your committee? What's his name? Max, that's it.'

Sylvia spoke just too quickly, but too easily, when she replied, 'Max? . . . oh just the same. Witty, charming and probably completely unscrupulous.' Mark met her eyes over the candle. 'Why do you say that?'

'Just a feeling,' Sylvia said.

'Um.'

'And what does "Um" mean?'

Mark raised his glass again. 'Nothing. Nothing at all,' he said, and added, 'Do you realise this is the first meal we have eaten together, just the two of us, for ages.' *Resist, resist,* Sylvia was telling herself, but she couldn't. 'I can remember quite a few breakfasts . . . ' she said; a little thrust, waiting for his parry.

'They don't count,' he said.

'Well they should do', she retorted. 'When a man first meets you his greatest ambition seems to be to have breakfast with you. And after he has, it becomes the by-word for the worst aspects of marriage.'

Mark allowed himself just the slightest hint of a grin as She raised his foil. 'Now whose romantic streak is showing?' he said. 'And who's been asking you – for breakfast?'

Sylvia relaxed. This thrust she could deal with. 'As a matter of fact a very attractive young man, witty, charming.'

'And probably completely unscrupulous,' Mark said sharply.

'No! Mark! I was referring to our son Peter.'

A hit, a palpable hit. 'Oh I'm sorry,' Mark said quietly.

'I thould think so.'

Back in town at the Telfords' house the fencing was of a physical nature. Jenny was sitting on the sofa, bearing across her chest almost the entire weight of Peter, who was red in the face, and running his tongue around the inside of her lips. What he lacked in finesse, he made up for in enthusiasm, but Jenny was beginning to lose the control which she valued highly.

She forced him off, roughly, and paused to take three deep breaths, before asking, 'Have you got an ambition to squash me flat or something?'

'Far from it,' said Peter, moving away from her slightly, realising that he was unlikely to succeed, despite the optimism which her obvious response to his advances had given him. 'Far from it,' he repeated.

'True. The way you're going on I should finish up with a very big bulge indeed . . . '

This was a situation which Peter had forseen. With the smile of a quiz participant who knows the answer to a question before the questionmaster has completed it, he patted his pocket and said, 'Be prepared!'

Jenny stood up immediately. 'Then be prepared for a shock!' she said. 'I'm going home in a minute. I mean, how do you know your parents aren't suddenly going to walk in?'

Peter's flagging optimism was momentarily revived. 'Because they're in Dover . . . all night.'

Jenny faced him. 'I hope you didn't think that I was going to stay all night,' she said sharply.

'Of course not, but it's early yet,' he said.

Jenny was suffering from a mixture of emotions. She had surprisingly deep feelings for Peter. And she was equally surprised at the arousal that his attentions had produced. But she did not like to feel that in any way she might be the victim of a plot. 'Why haven't you gone with them?' she demanded.

Peter sighed, the sigh of a man who has been diverted from passion into trivial discussion. 'I'm going tomorrow. I told them we had a rehearsal of the group.'

He leaned back towards her and ran his fingers down her breast. Even as her nipples stiffened, she said, 'Oh Peter! Please no! I wish you hadn't told them that, it sounds so sordid . . . '

Peter was not only losing the war, but plainly losing the battle. A new stratagem was desperately needed. Perhaps honesty would suffice. 'Look I promise, scouts honour,' he said, 'that I will tell them that I behaved like a gentleman.' She smiled at that. It was a minor victory for him. Which she immediately removed. 'And will you? Will you calm down a bit?' she asked, in a way that brooked no alternative.

'I promise. On condition that you don't go.' She agreed. Peter's response was to take her hand and begin a gentle nibbling of her knuckles, whilst looking deep into her eyes. She removed her fingers from his teeth and said, 'Let's make some coffee, shall we?'

No such scenes of violent, frustrated passion were being enacted in the Dover cottage. There was an atmosphere of complete peace as Mark and Sylvia sat in the armchairs near the fire nursing their brandy glasses. The small logs had caught nicely and were sending flames up the chimney and slivers of red-hot wood into the fireplace. Each was enjoying the sense of well-being that the good food, the scent of wood smoke, mingled with the tingling vapour of the brandy, was giving them.

'This has been the nicest evening I can remember for a long time,' Mark observed.

'Me too,' Sylvia agreed.

'Now I am not going to be tearing around all over the place, we can do it more often. You will get down here as soon as possible, won't you, Sylvia?'

There was a gentle, but firm insistence in Sylvia's voice, when she replied. 'You're incorrigible Mark.' Her manner had become again that of the woman who has seen the same action, repeated time after time, made by her husband as though it were an original discovery. 'You invest in a lovely meal, wine and brandy, and you want your interest straight away.' Mark was irritated. Whether with himself or Sylvia, he could not tell.

'I just want us to settle, that's all.'

'Let's not talk about it tonight, Mark. Don't let's spoil everything.'

But Mark was not to be put off. There was so much in his life that was still unsettled, that he could not leave the most important part still vague and undecided.

'I don't see how your saying to your wife that you want her with you spoils anything.'

Sylvia took breath, rested her brandy securely on the

arm of her chair, and allowed her voice to change from the gentle, after-dinner relaxation that had characterised it to something firmer – a real discussion point.

'All right, if you insist; I am thinking of getting a job.'

Mark brushed this aside as irrelevant. 'You have a job on the Theatres Committee.'

'I mean a *proper* job . . . an executive job . . . '

And again he made that impatient gesture, brushing aside any decisions that she might make as infinitely capable of change. 'If that's what you want I am sure we can find you something down here,' he said.

She leaned forward in her chair and said, strongly, her volume increasing with every sentence, 'I don't mean a farm secretary, or filing forms in an insurance brokers. I want to use what skills I have. I would like a job in a theatre or something like that . . . '

And now his voice hinted that she was being ridiculous. 'But how are you going to do that?'

'Not in Dover certainly.'

And now they were back in their familiar situation: Mark as manager and Sylvia as a customer coming with a proposition for a ridiculous business venture. 'That's obvious. I mean, how do you think you can land an executive job in a theatre on the basis of eighteen months as an assistant stage manager when you were eighteen?'

'That's not all I've done. I've been on all sorts of committees and I really understand theatre finance if anybody does. And I have lots of contacts.'

'Like Max, I suppose,' Mark spat at her. 'And I suppose he can make a grant contingent on your being given a job.'

Sylvia was genuinely hurt by this remark. The conversation was moving on to increasingly dangerous ground. 'Mark! That's unforgivable.'

He contrived to apologise in a way that suggested that an apology was not in order.

'It is just *you* isn't it?' she said loudly. '*You* and *your* job. *Your* life. *You* want to go overseas. *You* want to be in Dover. But what about *me*. I won't have Peter long – and then what will I have?'

'Me.'

'But I won't, Mark. Because you've shown that I'm only

second. Well that's all right. We can make a marriage on that basis. But only if it's the same for both of us. I don't mind playing second fiddle to your job providing we both have the same score.'

Mark's tone had changed now from that of a man certain of his ground and pointing out the obvious, to that of a man genuinely worried at the implications of the conversation and not, perhaps, wanting to face them. 'But how can we have a marriage if you're in London and I'm in Dover?' he asked slowly.

'Well, if I decide to get a job we'll just have to find out, won't we?'

There was a long pause. The only sound was the crackling of the fire. The light had almost gone and they were visible only by the flickering red glow from the logs. Mark looked for a long time at the dancing patterns that raced up and down the charcoal surfaces. Then Sylvia stood up and put her brandy glass on the table. Again there was a pause before she said, 'I'm very tired Mark. I'll go up to bed. I am sorry about the evening. It was a marvellous meal.'

She waited for a reply but Mark was staring fixedly at the fire. She went slowly to the staircase and made her way almost to the top; then she turned back. 'I said I'm sorry.' Her voice was very soft.

Mark spoke without lifting his head. 'Yes.'

She stood looking at him for a long time before she asked, 'What are you thinking?'

Mark half-lifted his head and looked towards her. 'Nothing really . . . I've just decided to lend a farmer sixty-five thousand pounds.'

Sylvia waited a moment for more explanation, but Mark had nothing more to say that evening. She gave a tiny shrug of the shoulders, a last glance at her husband, turned and went on up the stairs.

Mark sat looking into the fire.

Chapter Three

Mark rang the bell and waited until Harry the messenger opened the door on its chain. For a brief moment Mark worried that he might not be recognised, that the empire that had become his since Tom Stetchley's departure over the weekend might be shut to him. But Harry bade him good morning, slipped the chain and opened the door. It was nine o'clock.

The morning bustle was well on the way. The accountant was setting out books on his desk, and one of the girls was putting a fat new roll of paper into the computer terminal ready for the business chatter that would continue until five in the evening. But with no pressure from the customers at the tills, the atmosphere, although busy, was calm. Paper-wrapped bundles of one pound, five pound, and ten pound notes were slotted into the drawers behind the counter and the old ones were placed in tidy piles to be given out first. Keith Everly was already looking over some material in preparation for the interviews and decisions of the day. After an exchange of good mornings and the recognition that they were on their own, Mark admitted to a slight headache as a result of Mr Stetchley's send off. He went through into his office, took his coat off, hung it up, and looked around. He was by now familiar with the room, but up until this moment had felt like an interloper. Tom Stetchley had been completely at home here, fitting into it as easily as the furniture. This was the process that Mark must now begin. He looked out of the window at the early traffic in the street and up at the sky in case he might see a gull, but there were none. There was a tap at the door and Julie came in with a cup of coffee. It was apparently Tom Stetchley's custom to receive this warm drink before giving thought to the balance sheets, and Mark was glad to continue it. As he sipped the coffee, Carol came in with a list of firms that he'd asked for – all the firms in Dover employing more than 100 people. She had also thoughtfully included the name of their bankers where she knew it. His first interview would be at 10.15 with a local builder, Mr Burton. Carol handed Burton's statements across to Mark and he thanked her for her efficiency. The account was substantially overdrawn, but by arrangement. Carol did not know why Mr Burton was coming in but she did know that at 11.15 he had an appointment to see Mrs Phillips who apparently came in regularly to say nothing about money but a great deal about budgerigars. Mark realised suddenly that he was now back in the territory where budgerigars might be more important than blue chip multi-nationals.

'Oh God,' he said. 'Have we got many of them?'

'Our fair share. I've got the golf club form here. I filled it in as far as I can. If you could complete it I'll get it off. And I also have Mr Stetchley's proposal for the Royal Cinque Ports Yacht Club, if you'd like to fill that in too.'

'There's nothing else I need for the moment. I would like to see the new girl and then Mr Everly, please.'

Elizabeth Cowley, a girl of about the same age as Peter came into the room and perched nervously on the edge of the chair.

'I expect you're feeling very strange and new,' said Mark, and she nodded. 'So am I,' he went on, 'but it's worse for you because I have worked in a branch before. I expect you are glad to be starting work. No doubt a lot of your friends haven't found jobs?'

Elizabeth was over-awed by the occasion. 'No – I mean yes – they haven't,' she said, and dried up completely.

Mark pretended not to notice.

'I hope you'll like banking. I expect the Personnel Office

will have told you all about the opportunities for everyone starting work in a bank. It really is true you know. *All* the top men in the Bank started just as you are, standing in front of a Branch Manager, at your age, wondering how on earth they were going to cope with all those thousands of pounds you've already seen. I expect that Personnel will have told you about the Institute exams too?'

This was something Elizabeth knew about. 'Oh, yes,' she said, 'I start next week at the Tech.'

Mark nodded his approval. 'Good. Well it's a slog I know, and most girls give up to get married and have families. But I do hope you get stuck in and pass them first. You can always come back. Don't worry, I'm not going to lecture you. I hope you'll be happy here and if you aren't please don't be afraid to come to me, will you?'

Elizabeth mumbled that she certainly wouldn't, although in point of fact she certainly would. Mark smiled benevolently at her, trying to reinforce the image that he was cultivating, of himself as a particularly intelligent and thoughtful Manager who would have no need to shout because his staff would respect his perspicacity. He ushered her out and asked her if she would be kind enough to ask Mr Everly to come in.

Keith Everly stood until Mark invited him to sit.

'This builder, Burton, he's got a £60,000 secured loan,' said Mark, 'and an overdraft of £25,000. That's a bit high isn't it?'

'Yes, it is rather. He had a £15,000 facility and a couple of weeks ago he asked for another £10,000. He wanted it to finish four houses. Mr Stetchley went to see him, but wasn't very happy about increasing the overdraft.'

Mark interrupted to say, 'No, he wouldn't be. But he notes the houses were almost finished. Just decoration and outside paths and things left, so his cash flow will be looking healthier soon, I should think.'

In the back of his mind whilst he was conducting the conversation Mark was beginning to form an assessment of Keith Everly. The previous days that he had spent in the Bank had been directed more towards Tom Stetchley, but now he had to form an opinion of how best he could work with his assistant. Whether or not he was as ambitious as Tom had suggested he would of course discover, but there was no doubt that he had all the information at his fingertips when closely questioned about this account.

'He does have a regular cash flow from his ready mixed concrete business,' said Keith. 'He makes it at his yard and has a good contract for a year to sell to the Harbour Board for their new quay.' That was as far as they could take the matter until Burton arrived to explain why he had asked for the meeting.

Everly went off to continue checking his accounts and Mark began ringing some of the Managing Directors on the list that Carol had given him. He introduced himself to them and asked if he might call on them for a brief meeting. Many of them pointed out that they banked elsewhere, but Mark was determined that there should be no one of any significance in business in Dover whom he had not yet met. He wanted them, as he explained, to feel that if they ever did need a little extra finance they would not be talking to a complete stranger if they came to him. He was notably contented as he made the calls, extending his network into the town, hearing local voices, making himself known to them. He was interrupted by the unannounced arrival of a customer. The Reverend Kenton had called in on the off-chance that he might have a word with the new Manager. Mark readily agreed, and after a few moments he went to the public door of his office, looked through the spy hole in time to get a distorted close up of a clerical collar, pulled the bolt, and let the vicar in.

'It's good of you to see me without an appointment,' said Kenton. He was a tall man with a narrow face and an air of professional kindness and modesty. Mark could also detect an intelligence and sense of humour behind the grey-green eyes. Mark showed him to the chair, and remarked on the beauty of the church.

'You've been inside?' Kenton asked.

Mark mumbled his apology at having omitted this vital journey from his preliminary investigation of the town. He added even more apologetically that he was not a regular church-goer.

'Oh please,' said the Reverend Kenton, 'I haven't come to canvas your account, so to speak. It was just that I knew Tom Stetchley and I thought I'd pop in and welcome his successor to the town.'

Mark sat down behind the desk, and moved Burton's notes to one side. 'That's very kind of you,' he said. 'We call it "cold calling".'

Kenton said nothing but raised his eyebrows quizzically.

'It's what I'm doing now,' Mark continued. 'Getting my foot in the door of a local business, protesting that I don't want to poach their account, but hoping for the best.'

'Oh, I see. Well, I suppose we're both salesmen in different ways.'

'Very different. If your customers go spiritually bankrupt you don't foreclose on them, put in a receiver etc.'

Kenton smiled a sudden flickering smile as he came back immediately with the reply, 'Not exactly. There's no need you see. It's their loss, not ours.'

They began to labour this metaphor through paragraphs of prodigals, fatted calves, wayward sheep. Bank Managers as pastors, until the debate fell apart under a grave burden of biblical allusion. The Reverend Kenton rose to take his leave without disclosing the purpose of his visit.

'As a matter of interest, do we have your account?' asked Mark.

'Yes. Mine personally – and the church's for the time being . . . '

'That sounds ominous.'

The Reverend Kenton looked serious as he said, 'Well I would like to come and have a talk about our account fairly soon, if that would suit you. It's quite urgent, actually.'

Mark arranged to meet the Vicar for lunch and showed him out. As he was sitting down again and turning back to his lists, Keith Everly knocked and came in through the door from the clerical area of the Bank.

'Mr Telford,' he said, 'we've just had a phone message from Mr Burton's secretary. She says she's terribly sorry but he can't get to the appointment this morning. He'll ring for another later on.'

Mark said that it probably wasn't important, but Keith handed him a cheque which had come in that morning drawn by Burton for £5,000.

'Oh dear,' said Mark, 'well, I don't think we can clear this one. Do you?' Keith shook his head.

'See if you can get him on the 'phone. Tell him it's most urgent we speak to him within the next half hour,' said Mark.

Mark was as reluctant to make the call as Burton was to receive it. Burton said he was sorry that he wasn't able to come in but something had cropped up and he just couldn't make it.

'Yes, we got that message,' said Mark, 'but unfortunately something has cropped up here, too. Like a cheque drawn by you for £5,000.'

Burton hesitated before replying. 'Well, I negotiated an extra £10,000 overdraft.'

'Yes Mr Burton, but you must be aware, at least I hope you are aware that you have already drawn £8,000 of that.'

Again there was a measurable hesitation before Burton said, 'It's only £3,000 over. You surely wouldn't embarrass me with my suppliers for just £3,000.'

There was no hesitation from Mark whatsoever. 'Well it's £3,000 over the £10,000 which was £10,000 over the £15,000. There does have to be a stop somewhere, Mr Burton. But it's very unsatisfactory dealing with this over the 'phone when we've never even met. I'll come out there right away to see you.'

Burton argued that would not be necessary, but Mark was insistent. He would be there in half an hour and he made it quite plain that he expected to see Burton immediately.

Keith Everly said nothing but handed Mark's coat to him and helped him on with it.

'I'm afraid I shall have to leave my 11.15 interview to you Mr Everly,' said Mark.

'Oh that's all right,' said Everly with an eager manner that confirmed Tom Stetchley's analysis. Mark realised at that moment that Everly would be happy to conduct all the interviews and make all the decisions, and that Mark's sole function as far as Everly was concerned was to be some kind of experimental animal. By observing him Everly would enhance the skill with which *he* would respond to questions when he was interviewed for a Manager's position.

'A Mrs Phillips,' Mark added.

If Everly seemed a serious young man, this was given the lie by the smile with which he greeted Mark's revelation.

'You'd be surprised how often Mr Stetchley also found a pressing appointment when Mrs Phillips was coming in,' he said.

The taxi arrived for Mark sooner than he expected, and that fact together with the unusually light traffic would take him to Burton's yard sooner than he wished. Spotting Brook's supermarket, he asked the taxi driver to stop, and went inside. It was very busy. Several French housewives were filling their large shopping baskets with butter and other products that as yet had not risen to match Common Market prices. The owner of the supermarket, Mr Brook, was giving them every assistance and the two girls on the tills were hard at it ringing up the takings. Mark introduced himself to Brook, and said that Tom Stetchley had told him what a thriving business the supermarket was. Brook shook Mark's hand eagerly and said that it was strange that he should call in, because he had been intending to visit Mark at the bank. It was just a routine question. His accountant had told him that he ought to form a company and had said that there would be real tax advantages. Brook needed to open a company account.

'Daft isn't it,' said Brook. 'Crackers! I mean I'll have to work so much harder.'

Mark was surprised. 'Oh, Why?'

Brook laughed, 'I can't abide slackers. Anyone who works for me has to work hard.'

Mark was still chuckling over this as Brook showed him around the store. It was small but compact, and every inch was in use. Tins, bottles and packets were tightly stacked on the shelves and Mark wondered whether a pregnant woman pushing a trolley could have got along the narrow aisles and still find room to reach the merchandise. But Brook had plans to extend. He took Mark through a door at the back of the shop and showed him a crowded stock room.

'I'm going to convert this into a sales area and build a store room on to the back,' he said. 'There's about thirty yards of land doing nothing out there.'

'Will you be doing that soon?' Mark asked.

Brook nodded. He had the plans drawn, but he had been so busy, he had not had time to sort it out.

'Well,' said Mark, 'if you need any help in financing it you know where we are.'

'Right, I'll be knocking on your door,' said Brook.

Mark looked at his watch and decided that it was time to continue on to the builder's yard. Brook conducted him through the obstacle course of French housewives. Two of them had trollies so stacked with butter and legs of lamb that they needed all their effort to push them.

'Don't know how they get them past their customs,' said Brook.

The builder's yard was like any other, liberally coated with cement dust. Mark left the taxi at the gate, and walked in over the rough grey entrance, treading carefully around the little hillocks of concrete, and the chippings which were sprinkled like giant confetti. Through the window of the office he could see a man who he presumed was Burton, combing his hair. Mark took his chance to assess the efficiency of the yard. Two concrete mixers stood against the wall and there was a stack of timber in one corner, some of it plainly taken from the demolished buildings. In the centre of the yard was a lorry with a large drum in place of its platform. Beside the lorry a compressor stood silent and the high pressure line and the pneumatic drill were lying on the ground under the mouth of the drum. The back of the lorry had a ladder that led up to the drum. A woman of about thirty, with tousled blonde hair, came striding across the yard. She looked worried. She introduced herself to Mark as Pat Burton.

Burton himself followed her out of the office. Mark shook hands with him, but was making no effort to appear pleased that the interview was taking place in this dusty yard, rather than his own office. He asked Burton immediately for a tour of inspection. They looked into a store that was crammed with builder's supplies. There were heaps of gutters, drain-pipes, lavatory bowls, shelving, shelving-brackets, and floorboards. But there was none of the air of dilapidation or neglect that Mark had seen at Hetherington's Farm. All the supplies were neatly stacked and well ordered.

'You carry a large stock,' Mark observed.

'Well with inflation, it's money in the bank isn't it?' replied Burton.

'Unfortunately not. I'm afraid the interest you're paying on the money you borrowed to buy this lot is most probably higher than the rise in prices. And you do seem to have rather a lot of shelving.'

Burton nodded. Despite the circumstances, he was not making a very great effort to be charming. 'Yes, well, it's a trading town isn't it?'

They came out of the store and Mark strolled towards the lorry. Burton seemed eager to get him to the office and said that there would be some coffee waiting. Something in his manner alerted Mark.

'That's your concrete lorry is it?' he asked.

'Yes that's right. We make the concrete down the road.'

'And your compressor?'

Again Burton tried to edge Mark away from the lorry towards the office. 'No . . . We've no need of one much . . . cheaper to hire,' he said.

Mark left Burton's side and walked to the back end of the lorry, taking care not to soil his coat on the oily mechanism of the compressor. He went to the ladder, put his foot on the rung and completed the climb to the open mouth of the concrete drum. He looked inside but it was dark. And he was forced to put his head inside the grey, dusty opening to examine the contents. As his eyes grew accustomed to the darkness, his suspicion became a certainty. The drum of the lorry was full of concrete that had set hard. There were signs that Burton was engaged in the laborious task of breaking up the concrete with a pneumatic drill. Mark pulled his head back from the opening, and looked at Burton. Burton dropped his gaze down to the ground. He looked very miserable.

'Yes, well I think I could use that coffee now,' said Mark, as he stepped down on to the ground.

At least the coffee was hot. Pat Burton, if possible looked even more depressed than her husband. The office was small but tidy. A trader's calendar hung on the wall, and she had made an effort to make it more cheerful with a small vase of flowers. But Jack Burton, pacing up and down, his overalls thick with concrete dust, was a brooding figure. Mark said little, but Burton suddenly released his resentment at the misfortune that life had dealt him.

'The bloody idiot!' he said, slamming his fist on top of the filing cabinet. 'I only set him on on the Monday. He broke down. I was up on the site and Pat was out shopping. He said he couldn't get through to anyone so he just sat there at the side of the road. By the time I got there it was too late. Gone off. Set hard. It has to be a heavy mix for the quay, and you don't have a lot of time. Of course the first thing I did was sack him.'

'So you haven't been able to deliver concrete and all your expensive plant's standing idle?' said Mark.

Jack Burton and Pat exchanged glances.

'That's the point you see,' said Burton. 'I installed silos and mixers. I couldn't lose that contract . . . It's money every month you see, and I have to pay off the silos and so on. If I had lost just a week, I would have lost the contract, you see. There's enough firms who would love to pick it up. And you can't blame the Harbour Board's contracter. I mean he's got dozens of men down there shuttering and he's got a deadline . . . '

His outburst died away. 'So what did you do?' Mark asked.

There was a long pause. Jack looked at Pat and Mark noticed her look away.

'I bought another lorry,' Burton said.

Mark's exasperation showed in his voice. 'You bought another lorry? For eight thousand pounds? Using the money the Bank lent you to finish the houses . . . '

All Burton's anger at his situation returned. 'I had no option!' he shouted. 'If the concrete business folded I'd be finished anyway, with that expense of silos. I need a year's steady work to pay that off – and I've got it, there's no problem about that . . . '

'You should have come to us,' Mark said shortly.

'And would you have lent me another eight thousand?'

Mark looked out of the window at the silent yard. A great deal of money was doing nothing. And Mark was coming to the conclusion that there was no way that he could avoid bankrupting Jack Burton. It was a depressing start to the day.

'You can't insure against mechanical breakdown,' Burton went on, 'and even if you did the premiums would take all the profit. If you intend doing a job like the quay, believe me, you have to cut your costs to the bone to land the job. Nobody does anybody any favours. If you'd lend me the money I could set a couple of chaps on chipping the concrete out of the lorry. Otherwise *I've* got to do it, and what with everything else it will take at least a couple of weeks.'

Mark was totting up the figures for all this in his head. 'Will you be able to sell it then?' he asked, looking across at Pat Burton, in whose expression it was easy to see that she had detected the vultures on the skyline.

'I suppose so. It's not too bad. It should fetch . . . Well . . .'

Pat Burton turned round, moved towards her husband and said, desperately, 'Oh Jack, tell him! We can't go on like this, living from minute to minute! I'd rather pack it all in and go bankrupt.' Burton said nothing but hung his head and looked like a starved dog. Pat Burton turned her attention to Mark. There was more than a slight accusation in her voice. 'You don't know what it's like,' she went on. 'You work every hour, every second and then a machine breaks, then it's the weather, or people who don't pay their bills, It's not worth the bloody candle!'

She burst into tears, stood looking from Mark to Burton and then turned away and hurried from the office. Mark got up from his chair and closed the door after her. Her outburst was bringing home to him all the implications of that lorry full of misplaced harbour wall sitting in the yard.

'You'd better give me the whole picture Mr Burton,' he said more sympathetically.

Jack Burton slumped into a chair, picked up a pencil and stabbed aimlessly at an invoice that was lying on the table by his coffee cup.

'The police got to the lorry before I did. They got out a Ministry examiner and they issued a G.V.9 . . . *and* they're reporting me for having an unsafe vehicle on the road, so that'll be another couple of hundred up my shirt.'

'What's a G.V.9?' Mark asked.

'That's a certificate banning the vehicle until certain repairs are done.'

'So how much is it worth?'

Burton laughed without a hint of humour. 'As it is? Two and a half thousand. Maybe three. It's had it. I'll only sell it to a builder whose got less capital than I've got, if any such bloody fool exists.'

This additional information hardened Mark's tone again. 'So you bought new machinery to make concrete and a totally inadequate vehicle to deliver it.'

Jack Burton's manner was now that of a man standing in the dock accused of a crime he was prepared to admit so long as all the extenuating circumstances were taken into account. 'I bought the best I could afford,' he said. 'It only had to last a year till the heavy repayments on the silo and machinery were over. It lasted 5 months. So I still need £10,000 to finish the houses and I need the concrete mixing plant and lorry. Most of what's left is concreting and decoration of course.'

Mark thought for a moment making a mental tally. 'And this cheque for £5,000?' he asked.

'General supplies for the houses.'

Mark examined the cheque again. It was made to East Kent Building Supplies. If Burton did not pay, then he would not be able to obtain materials to finish the houses from any supplier in Kent.

'How much do you owe them?' Mark asked.

Burton said he would owe them nothing if Mark would only clear the cheque. But Mark insisted that Burton must owe them more than that. Surely no bill would come to exactly £5,000. Was this a part payment?

Burton looked at Mark with a new respect. He owed East Kent Building Supplies £8,650.

'So you need £10,000 to finish the houses and you owe £8,650. That's nearly £20,000,' said Mark.

'If you clear that cheque I won't need that, I can get what I need on credit.'

Mark sighed. It was a textbook case. 'You're over-trading Mr Burton. You're trying to act like a major contractor but with no capital. You've expanded much too quickly.'

Burton's voice was very bitter now. 'So you'll bust me. Put in a receiver?'

'Wouldn't that be a relief in fact?' Mark asked quietly.

'Would it hell!' Burton shouted, slamming his fist on the table. 'I'd lose everything wouldn't I? Every bloody thing I've worked for. After all this, saving up to buy the concrete business, the houses, the yard, I'll be back with a trowel in my hand. And just because some idiot left the concrete in the drum! He'd have done better to have shot the lot in the middle of the road! Oh, what's the point of all this! Why don't you just get it over with! Are you going to clear it or not?'

Mark stood up. 'I don't know,' he said. 'Let me be perfectly frank Mr Burton; on what I know now there is no way I can clear this cheque. And I either have to clear it or return it today. However I'm unwilling to put in a receiver if there is any way we can avoid it. I want you to collect up all your books and records. I remember your wife said something about bad debts?'

Once again Burton laughed in that dry humourless manner. 'I'm a builder aren't I? Whoever pays a builder until he's sued?'

'All right,' said Mark. 'I need some time and I've got a lunch appointment at 12.30. Could you be in my office at half past one? I can't say definitely that it will help. But if you press me now I'll have to refuse to pay this cheque. However it may well be worth just looking at the books and giving it an hour or two more.' Burton agreed to his suggestion.

Mark rang for a taxi and there was an embarrassed silence in the office until it drew up outside the yard. As Mark was getting in to it he heard the stuttering noise of the compressor starting and then the loud ringing thump of the pneumatic drill as Burton chipped hopelessly at his lorry full of stone.

Sylvia was nervous. Her decision in principle that she needed a proper job was fine as a principle but worrying when it came to implementation. Max had suggested that there might be an opening for her with a West End Manager called Tim Hart. He had suggested that she give

Tim Hart a ring and arrange a meeting. It took her 36 hours to pluck up the courage to do this but eventually she had made an appointment. It really was a major decision for her. There could be no turning back, she realised, once she had accepted any appointment that was offered – not that she saw much prospect of this becoming reality – because she had made her position quite clear to Mark and to retract from it would seem a terrible weakness. Not only that, but she felt strongly that Mark had acted unfairly and needed to be shown that she was a person as well as a wife. Despite this, her resolve was weakening as she pottered about the kitchen. The doorbell rang and when she answered it she was surprised to find Max standing on the doorstep.

'I was passing by and thought I'd . . . drop in . . . ' he said.

They went through to the lounge. Max explained that he had been at the Regent trying to work out how the theatre had managed to over-spend £5,000 on a budget of £10,000.

'And now you're going back to the office?' she asked.

He nodded.

'You ought to buy an A-Z. I know I'm only a simple Scottish lass but are you sure there isn't a quicker way from Soho to Piccadilly than via Islington?'

Max decided to come clean. 'Actually I thought I'd let you know I had a call from Tim Hart and I also wanted to tell you that I've got to go to the North for a month. Tomorrow.'

Sylvia frowned. 'That's short notice.'

Max explained that illness had necessitated his replacing a member of a team surveying the North. He was looking forward to it, he said.

'Except,' he went on, 'I'll be sorry to miss the last meeting with you.'

'Oh Max! I haven't even got the job yet and I don't suppose I will.'

'Don't under-value yourself Sylvia,' he said wagging a finger at her in a school-masterly manner. 'I've been thinking about our conversation and I've been worried about you. You know, if you take this job it could damage your marriage.' She made to interrupt, but Max continued, 'It's probablv interfering of me, but I felt I had to say it. You have every right to tell me to mind my business and bugger off . . . It's a strange thing, a marriage. Each one has it's own breaking point. For one it could be a single act of adultery. For another a forgotten birthday. Another could survive adulteries on a grand scale and a total memory blackout on anniversaries of all kinds. What's yours?'

'A gin and tonic I think,' Sylvia said and went across to a row of bottles. 'What will you have?'

Max accepted a whisky. Sylvia sipped her drink and said, 'The problem about a breaking point is that you don't know you've reached it until you've passed it. How did your marriage break up, if you don't mind my asking?'

'Died of neglect I suppose. Usual story of drift. Suddenly an exciting man came along and Mary realised she was only half alive.'

Sylvia nodded. 'Perhaps it would have been better if she'd got a job?'

'She did. She met him there. In the Inland Revenue office, would you believe.'

Sylvia was thoughtful. She swirled the ice in her drink. How much could she tell Max? What were his real intentions? He was behaving in a way that far transcended the duties of a committee chairman. Could she put this down to friendship? Sexual interest? Or was he just one of that nearly extinct breed, the gentleman?

'Well, I've always thought of my marriage as a shield. It's been very secure,' she said.

Max was very definite in his reply. 'I'm sure. From frontal assault. But taking a job – a real job – involves pushing it away a little, so that you can engage with people you are working with. And then it allows arrows in on the side. I know one man at least with his bow ready.'

At this last remark his voice had dropped and he was looking down into his whisky. The light from the window caught the smooth grey temples and gave him a strangely wise appearance.

Sylvia tried to reply lightly, but there was a hint of the coquette in her voice as she asked, 'Max are you offering to pierce on the side, so to speak?'

Max's voice came back to its full rich tone. 'Your heart! Oh no! I wasn't aiming that high.'

'Max!'

At last the subject that had remained with them like the fog on their night time drive from Celia's dinner was cleared and brought into the open. They laughed quite easily together.

'There's one thing I could do,' said Max. 'I could give you a lousy reference to Tim Hart.'

'Max!' Sylvia exclaimed. 'If you did that I'd . . . I'd . . .'

'Cut my throat!'

Sylvia leaned across the table and looked him in the eye. 'Oh no!' she said, 'I wouldn't be aiming that high either!'

And they laughed again.

Mark brought Keith Everly up to date with his discoveries about Burton.

'It's a lousy start,' he said. 'First day in the office and I bankrupt a local firm.'

'It's not your fault if he hasn't been levelling with us,' Keith Everly replied.

Mark asked Keith to tell him everything that he knew about Burton; every detail that might be useful. Burton had repaired Keith's roof and that had been very satisfactory, but then as Keith pointed out they were his bankers and could expect a good job. Burton's reputation seemed good. Keith had not heard anything against him.

'If he could finish those houses we'd get more of our money back than if we join a queue of creditors,' Keith offered.

'Of course. But can he finish them? Will he finish them, or will another few thousand find their way into some other enterprise? We are already extended as far as the security will go. By the way, I saw that the £100,000 for the yard was fully secured. What exactly is the security?'

Keith Everly sighed. 'There's the yard itself and his own house.'

Mark was genuinely distressed. In the world of international finance, companies are swallowed and digested in seconds and vast bankruptcies occur with no personal threat to the directors of the money invested in them. But rarely in the world of international finance did a simple decision imply that a man and his family would be turned out of their house. 'Oh my God,' Mark said.

They could go no further because the Reverend Kenton had arrived for his lunch appointment, but Mark asked Keith to go very carefully over Burton's statements and see if he could find anything, any tiny detail, that was not obvious.

The Reverend Kenton was a pleasant companion, and Mark enjoyed debating with him the question of South African investment. The Vicar and presumably his flock were incensed at the thought that the £111 which they had entrusted to Knight's Bank might be used to aid the machinery of exploitation in South Africa. But he was impressed with Mark's argument that the Bank was winding down its financial activities in South Africa, because it could not afford to jeopardise the potentially larger markets in the developing African countries North of the Zambezi. In the back of Mark's mind as they sipped their coffee was the feeling that, whereas the Vicar at this moment was seeking to protect people from the harmful effects of the society in which they live, Mark was on the brink of a decision which would bring personal disaster much nearer home.

Mark was late leaving the restaurant and returned to the Bank to find Burton sitting outside his office clutching in his arms a dozen ledger books, and a stack of papers stapled together. They went straight into the office. Carol interrupted briefly to tell him that Sylvia had rung but had not left a message. She shut the door after her.

Burton was now wearing cleaner clothes and had made another effort to remove the concrete dust from his hair and skin. 'Well what have you decided?' he asked.

Mark took breath and said, 'I've decided that I cannot extend the bank's position any further.'

Burton jumped up from his chair and shouted, 'So I've wasted my bloody time coming down here have I? Do you enjoy this or something?'

Mark tried to calm the atmosphere down a little. He said he would try if possible to find a way for him to continue trading without the Bank lending any more money. But he must either clear or return the cheque for £5,000 within 2 hours. They ran over the figures again.

'Now you need, I reckon, £13,000 to continue trading. That's £10,000 to finish the houses and £5,000 to pay to the suppliers and you have £2,000 left of your overdraft facility. Now how much is owed *to* you?'

'£5,000.'

'Realistically,' Mark went on, 'if you put them in the hands of a collecting agency, how much would you get?'

Burton thought for a moment, '£3,000 is pretty safe. I'd say the rest is problematical. But I don't need £10,000 to finish the houses. If I pay £5,000 to East Kent Building Supplies I can get credit from them again. So I need say £5,000.'

Mark was not happy with that assessment. 'No,' he said. 'You need £8,000 – and you might get £3,000 fairly quickly but we can't rely on it.'

Mark picked up the sheaf of papers and began leafing through them searching for a few figures which he thought might be significant. 'It was pretty obvious this morning that you were over-stocked. You must have thousands tied up in stock. 'Can you get rid of any of it?'

Burton was now out of his depth and becoming exasperated again. The urgency of his situation, and his realisation that the gamble that he had taken had not paid off, was moving him from the ability to make quick decisions into a muddled depression. 'Well how?' he asked, 'Unless I get another job and then I'd need credit for months before I was paid.'

If Burton had known Mark better he would have realised from the frown that crossed his face that a new thought had occurred to his new Bank Manager. He was about to continue but Mark ignored him and stood up.

'Just a minute Mr Burton. Would you mind waiting there. I won't be long,' said Mark. He went through the door from his office and shut it behind him. He walked past Carol's desk waving her to sit down again when she stood up, and went straight to the girl who was operating the computer terminal. He asked her to get him an immediate print-out of Mr Brook's account. He stood by her as she checked the code number for the account, typed it on to the terminal, and waited for the distant machine to whirl its tapes and come up with the information. While he was waiting Mark glanced along the counters to make sure that everything was in order. It was. The fact that no one seemed to be moving very quickly but there were no long queues of waiting customers clutching their cheque books and cheque cards told him that everything was under control.

The terminal chattered into life and began to print out a summary of Mr Brook's account. His current account showed only £800 in credit. But a deposit account held £8,640. The clerk ripped the print-out from the computer terminal and handed it to Mark. He smiled his thanks and after checking the figures over again he slipped the paper into his pocket and went back into his office. Burton was still sitting wrapped in gloom.

'I've had an idea,' said Mark. 'It's a very long shot, I'm afraid, but would you be prepared to wait for ten minutes or so?'

Burton would have been prepared at this juncture to wait all day. He shrugged. 'All right,' he said.

Mark asked Carol to get him Brook's supermarket on the telephone, and waited impatiently until his call came in.

'Ah, Mr Brook? Mark Telford here . . . from Knight's Bank. I wondered if I might have a quick word with you . . .'

At his supermarket Brook was rushed but cheerful. 'Now, Mr Telford. What can I do for you?'

'Mr Brook. You said that you were setting up a company to run the supermarket.'

'That's right,' said Brook. 'Next Monday, it starts.'

'Now, no doubt your Accountant has explained to you that as soon as you cease trading as a self-employed trader *all* your tax for the last 3 years is re-assessed and it becomes due immediately.'

Brook nodded. 'He told me it would come to about £5,000, but it's all right. I've been very careful about it. I've saved it up religiously. You ought to know. It's in your bank.'

Mark agreed. 'Did he also tell you that you ought to pay as many bills as you can before Monday to minimise the tax due?'

Brook was too good a businessman not to have thought

of that. 'Everything's paid up,' he said.

'Well, I've had an idea,' he said. 'I have a customer, a builder, who has a lot of stock he wants to get rid of. If you bought from him say £4,000 worth of stuff and paid him before Monday, it would reduce your tax due by at least £2,000. Of course you'd have to lay out the £4,000 now, but over the next few months you'd save at least £2,000 that wouldn't go to the tax man.'

Mark instantly went up in Brook's estimation. This was a very smart move indeed and had great appeal for a man who dealt in bargains. He gestured to the door. 'Wheel him in!' he said.

'Just a moment,' said Mark. 'Understand clearly you are not engaging him to build your extension. You must put that end out to tender as normal – but with the material here already that will lower the price. Of course, the same builder *may* put in the lowest price – in which case fine. But you are only buying stock, not engaging a builder. Now, if for *any* reason you'd rather wait to do your extension please don't agree to this. Don't feel pressurised by me whatever you do.' There was no hesitation in Brook at all. Having seen the bargain he was not going to relinquish it that easily. 'Oh no! I'm delighted. I really want the space.'

Mark was pleased. Perhaps his idea would work. 'Good,' he said. 'The builder's name is Mr Burton.'

'Oh, I know Jack Burton,' said Brook agreeably. 'He fitted those shelves. First class man.'

Mark was now very pleased. 'Better than ever,' he said. 'He's in my office. I'll send him down right away if that's all right, to look at the plans.'

Brook was plainly delighted. 'That's fine, yes, and thank you very much Mr Telford. It's not often a Bank Manager gives you a couple of grand.'

'Ah,' said Mark, 'It's not me giving it to you, it's the Chancellor of the Exchequer.'

By the time Mark arrived back in his office, Burton had half-filled the ashtray with stubbed out and broken cigarettes. His previous gloom had now mutated into nervous anxiety. Sitting in Mark's quiet office with only the sounds of chattering computer terminal and the low conversation of the bank clerks to distract him, he had been running over the possible futures that faced him. He realised that he had over-played his hand, but he was also aware that he might have succeeded in moving his money around, robbing Peter to pay Paul, to secure a rapid expansion if that stupid driver had not abandoned the lorry load of wet concrete. But he was not essentially a gambling man. He was, he knew, a very hard worker who had never in his life obtained a penny without striving for it. It was a particular humiliation to sit in this neat, quiet office awaiting the judgement of a man who he felt sure did not know the meaning of a three to one mix and had never split a brick neatly across the middle in his life. There was a quality in Mark's voice that he found irritating. It was the assurance that comes from a particular kind of family and a particular kind of education and a particular feeling of comfort in precisely those environments that Jack Burton found alien and oppressive.

Mark rushed into the office, shut the door firmly behind him, and said immediately, 'I think I've found a way. You know Brook's supermarket, I believe . . . Well he's going to have an extension built. He's got the plans and he's agreed to buy up to £4,000 worth of stock from you and pay you before Monday.'

Jack Burton might have been expected to react with pleasure to this news, but on the contrary he was very angry. The smooth talking Mark Telford had now, it seemed, robbed him of what little dignity he had left. 'You mean you told him I was stuck for money!' he shouted.

Mark made soothing gestures. 'No, of course not,' he said. 'He's paying you quickly for his own reasons, which are his business, which I won't discuss with you any more than I'll discuss *yours* with *him*.'

Burton was mollified. He apologised.

Mark understood how he must feel and quickly turned the conversation back to the business details. 'I want you to go down there now, see the plans and sell him up to £4,000 worth of materials to be used in the extension.'

Jack Burton grinned broadly and got up quickly from his seat. Mark Telford was now talking sense and he would show him that he was after all a decisive and adventurous businessman. 'Right!' he said.

But Mark stopped him. 'Just a moment. 'I must make clear that you are *not* at this stage engaged as the builder, but just selling stock. After all Mr Brook ought to put out the job to tender. So you do understand that? The next thing is I feel I must protect Mr Brook as he is my customer just as much as you are. Therefore I want you to give me a copy of the bill and plans. I will have them independently checked out and if the prices are at all high I shall recommend to Mr Brook that he doesn't pay the bill. In which case I shall put a receiver into your firm immediately.'

Burton's confidence was returning by the second. He understood the line that Mark was taking. He shook his head. 'Don't worry, I wouldn't twist Tony Brook.'

'Obviously I don't think you will otherwise I wouldn't be doing this but you understand I feel duty bound to look after his interests.'

Burton muttered his thanks and said that he understood very well. Mark then asked if he might take the second lorry as an assigned security for the overdraft. Burton made as though to object to this but then realised that he had nothing to gain from arguing. They shook hands and Burton went out looking if not pleased with himself at least more optimistic than when he came into the office.

Mark sat back in his chair and breathed out, as though he had just run up a difficult hill and could now take pause to recover his composure. It was, when all was said and done, a neat balancing trick. But he thought to himself, *I must not give myself too much praise. If I had not walked into Brook's supermarket because I was early on my first visit to Burton, I would not have had the means to help him avoid bankruptcy.* Nevertheless, he allowed himself a small pat on the back for putting the two unrelated situations together to form a solution.

The telephone rang and Carol connected the Chief General Manager. He managed to avoid commenting on the fact that it was Mark's first day as his own Manager, and did not even ask him if he was enjoying this return to pastures old. He merely said that a party of people from Manton's, the French multi-national, would be coming to Dover the following week and he would like Mark to look after them and make sure they had all the information they might require. But he couldn't help adding, 'You'll be pleased to see them, I expect. Give you some excitement.'

Mark put the phone down and grinned. It would be a long time before Head Office would accept him as Mark Telford, the Manager of the Dover Branch, instead of Mark Telford of the International Division. But he also thought he was in a unique position to assist with Manton's operation. How many other Branch Managers would understand fully the requirements of a French-based firm?

Then he picked up the uncleared cheque for £5,000 which had sent him out on his morning mission to Burton's building yard. He carried it through, gave it to a clerk and watched it being stamped with the Branch stamp and initialled before going off to be cleared. That one simple action, which looked so insignificant, had changed the course of the Burtons' lives. Perhaps in 3 months, 6 months, 5 years, Jack Burton might over-reach himself again and find himself in the bankruptcy court. But for the moment he was safe.

Mark lifted his eyes from the desk and went along to ask Elizabeth Cowley how she was enjoying her first day. She smiled at him and said that it had been wonderful. He looked up through the armoured glass and to his amazement watched Sylvia walk into the Bank. He went quickly back through his own room, shut the security door and went through the public door out to greet her. 'Everything all right?' he asked, anxiously.

Sylvia cocked her head to one side. 'Yes, of course,' she said. 'Just thought I'd surprise you, that's all.'

'You've certainly done that,' he said, leading her through to his office, closing the door behind them and taking her coat.

'Well, it's nice to see you here,' he said.

'Yes.'

Something in the tone of her voice alerted him. Between people who have been married as long as they had there are many ways of communicating. One single word can mean twenty.

He went to her. 'What's the matter?' he asked.

'Nothing.' It was as though she wanted to say something else but couldn't bring herself to.

'Peter all right?' Mark asked, probing.

'Yes fine. In fact I've some good news,' she said in a way that implied some doubt. Mark raised his eyebrows. 'Yes,' she went on. 'I've got an interview for a job.'

Mark found himself sitting behind his desk. 'Where?' he asked in a slightly more peremptory way than he would ever have used with Burton.

'Tim Hart Productions. He's a very important theatrical manager; puts on all sorts of things in the West End. I shan't get it, of course, but just to get an interview is something, and it's . . .'

'In London,' said Mark.

Sylvia said nothing. Her look confirmed his assumption. Mark's gaze fell from her to the neat unmarked blotting paper on his desk. There was a very long pause. 'I see,' he said.

It was a brief phrase, but he contrived to express in it a mixture of hurt, anger, resignation and loss. This was the moment that Sylvia had been dreading. She had thought carefully about waiting until she knew whether she had or had not obtained the job before saying anything to him. But she knew that her mind was fully made up. The fact that she was going to an interview was sufficiently concrete a symbol of her state of mind, and their state of marriage, to make the actual job itself irrelevant.

This was why she had made the long and irritating journey to Dover, just to say those few words in person. But now the moment had arrived she was upset at having to examine Mark's face and see in it so much pain. True, he was at least as much to blame for this gulf as she, but now she felt guilty, and alone.

Mark sat behind the desk, not looking quite at home in the chair or the room, and she sensed his own loneliness. It was like a physical shock to her.

'Mark . . . please,' she said very gently, meaning, let's not go off into that blind alley of resentment and antagonism.

She could tell that Mark was not so much weighing the implications of her interview as deciding what manner of reaction he should make. And by that subliminal sensitivity which they had not yet lost, when he rose quickly to his feet and pulled open the drinks cabinet, she knew that he had decided on a *performance*; a dramatic gesture of erasure that would cover the more subtle feelings which she could read unmistakably in his face.

'We'd better celebrate then,' he said too cheerfully, making a great play of deciding which drink would be appropriate. He selected the bottle and took slow and patient trouble in pouring it into two glasses.

He strode round the desk and gave Sylvia her drink.

'Thanks,' she said softly, with not the slightest hint of any willingness to spar or score points.

Mark's cheerfulness was now overpowering. He raised his glass in a toast. 'Cheers! Here's hoping.'

She examined his expression for any clues as to what lay behind that remark. There were none, so she felt required to wrest it from him.

'Of course,' she said. 'But for what?'

'Whatever will make us both happy,' he said, still holding the glass aloft and looking into her eyes.

She raised her glass. They remained like that for a moment, a tableau, papering splendidly over the vast crack that was now separating them. 'I'll drink to that,' she said quickly.

Chapter Four

Mark took an early morning stroll in the summer sunshine along the cliff walk. Far below the surf beat angrily on the shingle, but its sound was a distant whisper. He stood for ten minutes watching the miraculous poise of a bird that held itself as a still point in the sky, twisting its wings at the tip just enough to keep it in balance in the turbulent breeze. He felt an affinity with the bird, perched high as he was on the brink of the land. Clouds were moving in from the channel. In the far distance a ferry was approaching Dover.

One of Mark's recurrent feelings at this time in his life was a fear that, despite his decisiveness, events were not quite within his control. He felt a curious surprise that he should be standing here on this cliff only half an hour's walk from his place of work. He was used to the rhythms of travel and hotel life. They seemed natural; the inevitable price that he had paid for standing in the fast currents of international finance and diverting them to the advantage of the Bank. But here, in this town which he had still not come to accept as his own, he had had to construct a new, lonely domesticity. Until now there had been travel and there had been home. Sylvia and Peter seemed further from him now than he had felt them to be when he was in Paris or Frankfurt or Cologne or Vienna. He was beginning to realise that his expectation of diverting the currents of their lives with one simple decision had been wrong. Had he erred so badly in the International Division he would have been demoted to a much more lowly position than the managership he had selected for himself. His meeting with Sylvia had made it quite clear to him that she would now make the pattern of her life according to *her* needs. He realised also that though his strategy might, as he was still convinced, have been correct, his tactics were appalling. As he stood on the breeze-ruffled grass watching the waves force themselves out of the sea to the point of breaking, he knew that Sylvia had taken a step which was not irrevocable as far as their marriage was concerned, but which had placed him at a point of decision. It was not too late for him to pass off his few weeks in Dover as an anomaly, as the results of exhaustion from which he was now fully recovered. Haslet would be pleased to have him return immediately to the International Division, and no doubt would have a meeting in Istanbul already booked for Mark by the time he arrived in London.

Damn it all! he thought to himself as he began the walk back down into the town, *Was it not unfair of all of them to expect that his life would go straight as an arrow to the obvious bulls eye that they had all predicted for him?* Surely a man was entitled to take stock in his 40's and weigh of course of the last 15 or 20 years of his working life? Because he had the ability and the drive and the judgement to act as an international operator, did that mean he was condemned for ever to wander like a lost soul in Hades to and fro across that dull green Styx that surged before him? He thought not.

Sylvia had been right to condemn him for not consulting her. But he was, after all, paid to be decisive. Decisions were natural to him; vagueness was not. But following that thought, came another. Was he right in assuming that all of life's activities could be conducted by the same criteria that defined the world of banking?

The thought was still in his mind as he dealt with the early business of the day in the Bank. He had an unpleasant start when he had to admonish a cashier who was slipping into a habit of persistent lateness. Then he had had to deal with a lot of boring administration. He tried to ring Sylvia but she had already left the house.

The Bank was not yet open to the public, so Mark was surprised when Charlie, the messenger, tapped on his door to say that a Mr Felpersham wished to see him urgently. Neither Carol nor Mark had heard of Mr Felpersham before.

'He says he's from the court at Canterbury,' said Charlie.

Mark asked Charlie to show Mr Felpersham in. He was a small man with grey hair and a neatly trimmed white moustache. He wore a charcoal-grey, pin-striped suit, a stiff collar and a silvery tie. He quickly established that Mark was the Manager of the branch and then handed Mark a paper sealed with wax.

'I'm a bailiff from Canterbury Crown Court, and I've been instructed to serve this order on you. It is a garnishee order attaching the account of Mr John Burton.'

Mark could not recall the details of a garnishee order, a fact which he would certainly not reveal to Mr Felpersham. He opened the paper.

Felpersham bade him good morning and left the office.

'What on earth is a garnishee order?' asked Carol.

'I have only the remotest idea. You'd better get Mr Everly in,' said Mark. He was still frowning at the impenetrable official language and legal jargon as Keith walked in.

'Morning Keith. You're nearer the Institute exams than I am. What on earth is a "garnishee order?" '

Keith Everly's eyes brightened with that surprised thrill usually seen only on the faces of anglers who have hauled nothing but weed from the waters for a week and now detect a threshing at the end of their line.

'Garnishee? Is that one there? How fascinating.'

Keith Everly moved round to look over Mark's arm at the document.

'I'm sure it is,' said Mark, 'when one knows what it is!'

'Oh dear,' said Keith, 'It's on Burton's account. It means that he didn't tell us everything.'

That much Mark had gathered for himself. The Plaintiff was East Kent Building Supplies and as Keith went on to explain to Mark, it meant that Burton was a judgement debtor.

East Kent Building Supplies at some time in the past had

got a court judgement against Burton for a certain sum. They checked through the pages of the document and found that it amounted to £212. Burton had not paid the bill and as a result the suppliers had gone to the court and obtained this garnishee injunction.

'It means we can't pay any cheques of his that come in until he pays that debt and the court revoke this order. What an idiot, for £212 and he didn't tell us about it,' Keith continued.

'I wonder how much more he didn't tell us about. Have we any cheques in from today?' Mark directed the question to Carol, and she went out to check through the stacks of uncleared cheques that were now being sifted by the staff.

'Difficult, isn't it?' said Keith with the air of a man who found nothing more bracing than difficulty. 'I mean, we're by far and away the biggest debtors and quite a bit unsecured. If we bounce all his cheques there'll be a bankruptcy petition before you can say knife, and we'd lose the most.'

Mark was particularly exasperated that Jack Burton should be the one to cause this difficulty. But he remembered from his previous experience as a manager that clients of the bank who were going through a period of difficulty rarely explained absolutely everything. There is a certain social stigma in implying that one has dealt unwisely with one's money. Mark had seen many others who had made his life unnecessarily difficult by not arming him with all the facts before seeking his advice.

'We can't go on like this,' he said. 'You'd better get on to him and tell him to get in here fast, before *I* put a receiver in. And as far as his cheques go, do what the judge says: bounce them.'

The thought of bouncing Burton's cheques caused only the most trifling flicker of remorse in Keith Everly. Dull pages of textbooks which he had recently read were springing into life for him. 'Let's hope there's none with a cheque card number on the back,' he observed.

Mark made it quite clear that he had not an inkling of Keith's meaning.

The Assistant Manager continued with his briefing. 'There was a fascinating discussion in the Banker's magazine a few months ago about this very point. If a cheque is given with a cheque card guarantee, does the Bank, in law, effectively pay on the cheque immediately it is given, instead of when it arrives in the bank?'

Mark waited in vain for the resolution of this fascinating intellectual problem. 'Well what's the answer?' he asked.

Keith Everly was delighted. 'Nobody knows! It hasn't been tested in court. Perhaps it will now!'

Mark wondered whether there was something the matter with him. He could not face the prospect of being a test case with the same unalloyed enthusiasm as his assistant.

When Carol came in with a bunch of Burton's cheques in her hand Everly took them from her without offering them first to Mark. He flicked through them quickly and

'Thank God for that,' said Mark. 'I'm sorry to disappointed. There were no cheque card numbers.

'Thank God for that, 'said Mark. 'I'm sorry to disappoint you, Keith, but the Dover branch isn't going to make legal history. Get Burton will you. I want him here. Now!'

The telephone rang and interrupted them. It was the Chief General Manager. 'How is it down in sleepy hollow?'

'Very nice,' said Mark with a smile. 'I've just woken up the elves, and the pixies are polishing the toadstools . . . and a very naughty pixie has just arrived from the Crown Court with a garnishee order on one of our customers.'

Even at this distance, through the crackling line, the note of interest in Harvey's voice was unmistakable. 'Do they still exist? I've never had to deal with one myself. Fascinating.'

Mark looked across at Keith. 'That's what my Assistant Manager says. He's enjoying it more than a birthday present.'

'How much is it for?' Harvey asked.

'£212.'

'What a piddling sum! Your Assistant good, is he?'

Again Mark smiled at Keith as though to include him in the conversation. 'Keen as mustard. He's already lectured me on all the points to be taken into account and he's now on to the legal department to tell *them* what a garnishee order is.'

Harvey dismissed the matter. 'Jolly good. So you can leave him to cope with it. I'd like you to come up for lunch, Mark.'

Mark frowned. 'This order may be for two hundred odd but a bankruptcy and a bad debt to us of £15,000 may hang on it.'

This was small fry to Harvey, for whom a million had by this time become a relatively small amount. 'Well, of course, I have to leave it to you, but Jacques Dupont of Manton's has just rung me. He is in town and thought a meeting would be a good thing. We're lunching him. And seeing that the main reason – in fact the only compelling reason – for letting you go down there was to look after Manton's, I thought it would be a good thing if you were to be here. *If* you can put a holding action on your little local difficulty, I would appreciate it if you could manage to make it. Of course, as I said, it's up to you.'

Mark could understand the importance of the meeting and reluctantly he agreed to be in London at half-past twelve to make a quick gesture to his previous existence. Mark looked at Keith thoughtfully. He was unwilling to leave the branch with this threat hanging over them, but at the same time it was obvious not only that Keith was keen to deal with the matter, but that he was far better versed in the technicalities of the order itself than Mark was. It would in a way be selfish of Mark to stay and insist on handling the matter himself. Keith Everly was paid to assist, and when necessary to deputise, and he could now do it.

'Look, you'll have to deal with Burton. Tell him we're stopping all cheques by court order. Chew him up. Show him he's really let us down. And for God's sake find out what other nasty surprises he's got in store for us. 'We may have to put a receiver in, but we need to know everything this time. If it is only a matter of £200 we shall probably wear it, but do impress on him this is absolutely his last chance. If he doesn't tell us *everything* he'll move so fast into bankruptcy he'll be invisible.'

From the reactions of the younger passers by in Greek Street it was plain that in her smart interview dress, which contrived to be elegant but also casual, Sylvia was anything but casual. She was a mixture of apprehension and excitement. She did not want to be early for her interview but could not settle down long enough to drink a cup of coffee. She glanced at her reflection in the passing shop windows and felt a sense of approval at her appearance. She looked at her watch again and decided it was time to make her way to Shaftsbury Avenue, where she found the right theatre and paused to examine again the peculiar spelling of the name of a northern writer of comedies. She went in through the foyer and was directed to Tim Hart's office at the booking desk. Through a little door she found a short white flight of steps. The walls were covered with scrappy theatre notices and invoices that had been hung there. Then she came to the iron grille of a lift, one of those Edwardian-seeming arrangements which requires good muscles and determination to move back the heavy lattice-work. When she had negotiated the doors, she found the narrowest lift she had ever seen, so tight that her hips nearly touched it on each side. She heaved the grille to and pressed the button. The lift cranked unwillingly into action. It had a grinding, juddering motion that together with its cramped proportions Sylvia found mildly distressing. Grey walls descended slowly past the grille. Here or there graffiti has been scrawled quickly by some adventurous soul who was fast with the felt-tip.

The lift clanged to a halt and vibrated gently as though panting after its exertions. She opened the gates and went through to make herself known to the secretary.

The office seemed well appointed. Large theatrical posters hung in neat frames on the walls, which were impeccably white. The furniture matched perfectly. A low glass coffee table stood between black leather chairs. A low shelf was graced with miniature palms, their leaves an even and healthy green. The secretary announced her arrival to the intercom.

Tim Hart was probably about forty-two. He was immaculately dressed in a blue suit and wide-knotted floral tie. His hair was a light shade of brown in contrast to his surprisingly dark eyes. He was well built, nicely proportioned, with the slightest hint that without care he might put on an unwanted pound or two. He looked as though he would worry about each ounce of those pounds. He smiled a welcome, shook her hand, and showed her into another office. He called back to Pat, the secretary, and asked her if she would be kind enough to bring in two cups of coffee.

The inner sanctum was, if anything, more elegantly furnished than the outer vestibule. Tim Hart's desk was wide without seeming ostentatious. His chair was hardly that of a man who would sit hunched over his books. It suggested rather a tendency to lean back and think elegant thoughts. Nevertheless, it was not the office of a playboy manager. Everything in it, although beautifully designed, had a function. He held the back of an equally comfortable chair for Sylvia to sit down and invited her to make herself at home. He asked if they might talk to each other on first name terms, a request to which she readily agreed. Sylvia arranged her legs neatly and wondered if the slight flush she could feel from inside was discernible on the surface of her cheeks.

'So,' he said, 'you want to leave the cosy world of subsidised theatre and come out into the cold with us. Why do you want this job?'

If ever there was a time for the 'thrust and parry' approach this was it. 'I don't know that I do yet,' said Sylvia.

'Oh?' he said, raising his eyebrows.

'Well, if I'm to be your assistant I'd need to like you,' she said, 'and we haven't talked yet.'

Tim Hart leaned back in his chair and smiled at her over the cut crystal ash tray. 'Oh dear! It's me that's getting interviewed! I'm glad I wore a good suit!'

Sylvia immediately began an apology, but he cut across her and dismissed her apology lightly. 'O.K. let's play it like that,' he said. 'What do you want to know?'

It was definitely a challenge. She accepted it.

'All right? Why do you think you're a good employer?'

'Mmm! You don't muck about do you? Aren't you going to try and put me at my ease before getting to the nitty-gritty?'

It was a fair point but not one that Sylvia was prepared to accept. 'No,' she said. 'You're on your own patch. If you're not at ease already I'd rather not work for you.'

'Fair enough! Why am I a good employer? Mmm . . . well firstly I offer very interesting work to do. I've got three shows in town at the minute and we're working on another four. Secondly . . . I'm very clean and tidy . . . ' He held up his hands to display their sterile virtues. 'Thirdly . . . the money's not bad . . . and fourthly, I'm not a very conventional person and a life here is never predictable. I mean, I didn't know I was going for an interview myself this morning. So do I get the job?'

Sylvia was enjoying the interview. 'I have one more question,' she said.

He sat forward suddenly in his chair and opened his arms in a submissive gesture. 'Shoot!' he said.

Sylvia quenched her smile sufficiently to indicate that this was more than an empty remark. 'I have very little experience in the theatre, though quite a bit on the understanding of balance sheets, production budgets, and so on. However, I haven't been involved in, for example, casting, set design, and lots of other things. Why did you think I might be suitable for the job?'

And Tim Hart showed too that he could be serious. 'Well, I know Max Fielding, and he recommends you – highly. And, again, I think it more important to get an intelligent balanced person, who can learn the job, than maybe an experienced person who *may* be very set in her ways.' Tim sat back in his chair.

Sylvia nodded in a business-like way. 'Fine. You get the job of being my employer. All we have to decide is when you start.'

Tim Hart burst out laughing and slapped his hand on the desk with delight. 'Bloody marvellous! What can I say? You've completely pre-empted me. Well . . . how about a month's trial either side?'

Sylvia nodded her agreement. 'Thank you very much,' she said.

'Not at all,' Tim Hart continued, 'you'll want to see if I measure up to the job.'

The secretary brought in a tray of coffee and set it down on Tim's desk. As he poured it he said speculatively, 'Well as I know nothing about my new assistant, what are you doing for lunch?'

Sylvia had arranged to meet Celia Hawkins to give her

a blow by blow account of the interview, but she said nothing, and arranged to meet Tim at a restaurant called Angelo's.

Three miles away in the city Mark was joining Harvey, Haslet and Monsieur Dupont for lunch. Dupont had just been commenting that the county authorities seemed to be rushing the planning permission and all the other formalities through. He was delighted with the arrangements that Mark Telford had made. Harvey passed his compliments on to Mark when he came into the room. A waiter brought another round of the huge aperitifs that were obligatory in the upper echelons of the Bank. Dupont was fascinated by Mark's 'change of life', as he put it. Harvey and Haslet nodded sagely at each other and chuckled at what seemed to them an inadvertently excellent definition of Mark's state of mind.

'Are you enjoying yourself in Dover?' Dupont asked.

Mark said he was enjoying it very much and he was sure Manton's would be very happy there too.

'You must make the most of Mark Telford, Monsieur,' said Haslet, 'I make no bones about wanting him back in the International Division.'

Dupont waved his glass at Mark. 'But you are playing hard to get? . . . Eh Mr Telford?'

'Not at all Monsieur, I'm just doing what I want to do. Is that so revolutionary?' Mark asked.

Dupont was not a man to be bettered. 'Could be, after all, that was all Lenin was doing wasn't it?' he said.

'Telford is happy down in Dover with his garnishee orders, aren't you Mark?' Harvey asked, pointedly.

Dupont looked puzzled, and made a gesture to Mark inviting him to explain this unknown word.

'I'm sorry Monsieur Dupont,' said Mark. 'I'm afraid I don't know any more about it than you. My assistant's looking after it. He's an expert.'

'How's it going?' Harvey asked.

'I've just rung my assistant,' Mark said. 'He's getting our wayward client in this afternoon.'

* * *

Tim was already waiting, drink in hand, for Sylvia when she arrived at the restaurant. Sylvia was determined not to become so bloated by the lunch that she could neither think nor talk straight. She ordered *calamari* and a green salad. Tim Hart, plainly in need of sustenance, ate his way through a delicious *veal escalope Valdostana*, whilst contriving at the same time to talk about the business. Sylvia caught herself wondering idly whether this ability to speak with the mouthful of rich Italian food was an art that she would have to cultivate. The white wine was chilled and excellent.

Tim sipped, and said, 'After you'd gone, I sat there thinking, I don't know a damned thing about her and I've just hired her. Mind you, I've no regrets. I told myself, I do in fact know one thing about you.' She raised her eyebrows, but he continued, 'You are a damn good hustler and that's just what I need.'

'I hope that's a compliment,' she said, in a manner that made plain that it was.

'Depends on where you're sitting. In a theatre manager's chair it's essential, probably the most important thing. You have to begin by hustling yourself a play to do and beat down what the writer wants. You see he tends to think of his play as a bit of his soul and wants to sell it for the same money as Faust got for his . . . '

Sylvia feigned a slight shock. 'That casts us in the role of the devil,' she said.

'That goes without saying.'

At this moment a waiter came across to enquire if their food was satisfactory, and Tim extolled its virtues for a moment or two before continuing. 'Then you have to hustle yourself a star or two who also wants the earth, plus billing above the title of the play. If you're not careful, you get so many names above, the title has to appear as some sort of P.S. at the bottom of the poster.'

'What about the writer's billing?' she asked.

Tim paused with a fork full of veal. 'Ah well, you've got to remember that he's in the soul business, above all the petty haggling over billing, and would probably restrict himself to a pathetic little squeak when he first sees the poster . . . Then you have to hustle yourself a theatre in the sticks to start it off and another in town to bring it in.

You have to hustle as much publicity as you can, pay for as little as you can. And on top of all that you have to hustle enough bankers to get the play on at all. So what with all this you'll be very busy. What does your husband do?' He asked unexpectedly.

'He's a banker,' she said, trying not to make it sound like an affliction.

Affliction was certainly not the view that Tim took of the matter. 'Really! Well perhaps you won't have to hustle so hard for the money, then.'

'You're joking! They'll lend you money against security but they won't invest in speculative ventures.'

In response to Tim's gentle prodding, Sylvia gave a brief account of Mark's career and his peculiar behaviour of late. Tim filled his mouth sufficiently to give himself time for thought and then said very directly, 'Are you splitting up?'

Sylvia had not been expecting this question. She managed to reply quickly, 'Good Lord no! We'll probably see just as much of each other now as we did before, when he was flying all over Europe.'

'Good!' Tim said emphatically.

'Why "good"?'

'I don't know. I suppose I like unorthodox solutions to the usual boring problems. That's the whole secret of a good play. Spot that and you have a winner. I mean, you take a problem everyone has, say old age, get it a *particular* press, call it "King Lear", and bingo, you've got a winner. 'Or, "Shall I, Shan't I", and you've got Hamlet. I've always thought that play is the biggest commercial hit of all time because most everyone *is* indecisive.'

Sylvia mused over this. How many victories, she wondered, should she let him have? 'Mmm,' she said, superficially impressed. 'So why is it so difficult to spot the winners?'

Tim continued in his assured way. Sylvia was forming the impression that there was no question under the sun for which Tim Hart would not have a ready and articulate answer.

'Because the problem has to be commonplace, but the dress has to be *Haute Couture*, exclusive, one-off. And there aren't enough designers capable of that, so we have to use the next best and buy off the peg. Recognising a great play is easy. It jumps off your desk or it doesn't. It's finding a good one that's difficult, because it's a question of fine judgement, just like a dress. Now the neckline certainly is plunging; will it be enough to distract attention from the fact that shoulders don't quite fit, or the hem is slightly uneven?'

Sylvia nodded in agreement. 'Hence the spate of sexy plays.'

'Absolutely. Unfortunately, or fortunately, we've almost gone as far on that point as we can. The audience isn't distracted by a bare breast anymore, or even a full frontal, if it comes to that. So it looks as though we're going to have to find ourselves some really good plays to earn our crust.'

'I'll drink to that,' said Sylvia, raising her glass.

He clinked his glass against hers and they drank, both realising that the subject of the toast was something more than just a search for new plays.

Mark was also talking with a glass in his hand. The fact that he had in theory humbled himself and swung a few rungs down the ladder had in no way carried with it any change in his way of speaking. 'The great thing about life,' he was saying, 'is that you don't know when you are going to die. It's indefinite. It could be now, at this minute or in fifty years time, so for all practical purposes it's no good considering it. But my work has *been* my life so far, and that life has had its day of death decided. The year, the month, even the day. Our compulsory retirement may seem fine when you're thirty-five, but when you're forty-five it's an uncomfortable thought.'

Monsieur Dupont, who had only two years to go before his compulsory retirement at sixty, said, 'Perhaps uncomfortable enough to force you to give up your place on the ladder and to develop other sides to your life?'

Harvey and Haslet had said little during this conversation, and were watching Mark with that accounting gaze which he had seen them use at interviews. 'Well,' he said, 'it could be an unconscious motive I suppose, but really I was thinking more about the quality of my life *now.*'

'I hope so Mark, otherwise you've made the wrong decision,' Harvey suggested. 'All right, I have to retire from this job in a few years, but by God I'll get another. On a Board, or as a financial adviser, or representative for a foreign bank, or something. But there isn't that opportunity for every bank manager who retires.'

'No I realise that,' said Mark, 'but isn't there something odd about working every moment of your life, failing to explore all sorts of interesting avenues, so that you can get a good job when you're sixty?'

Dupont smiled gently into his claret.

If Mark had been able to look into his Dover office at that instant, he would have observed Jack Burton, the builder, slumped in his chair like a tangible echo of that moment when he had brought in his books for examination. Keith was now sitting in Mark's chair and giving Jack Burton a hard time. He ran over the many serious crimes of omission in Burton's accounts of his finances. When Burton said that he had forgotten about the two hundred and sixty pounds which had caused the suppliers to seek a court injunction, Keith reacted strongly. It was not the sort of thing that one should easily forget, and that was no excuse.

Despite his situation, Burton was still behaving like a man who was the victim, not of his own inefficiency or bad judgement, but of a conspiracy on the part of all those of whom Keith Everly seemed to be the co-opted representative. When Keith insisted that they must refer his cheques, Burton reacted cynically. If the bank wanted to pay, the bank could pay, despite the garnishee order. Technically this was true. The order was only effective when served on another debtor of Burton's, which the bank certainly was not. It was Burton who owed the bank money and not the other way round. But if they paid the cheques, they would merely be increasing his indebtedness to the bank and not paying out money of his that was frozen for another debtor.

'Then please do it,' Burton pleaded. 'If you stop those

cheques I'm finished. They're both to people who will put in the receiver *immediately* they get my cheques back. No doubt.'

Keith shook his head. He was quite definite, and in any case, he was acting on instructions from Mr Telford.

Burton brandished a cheque from Tony Brook, for four thousand pounds for the shelving. When that was paid in, surely Mr Everly would pay the cheques?

'It's a good job that Canterbury Building Supplies didn't know about Mr Brook or else he'd have received the order,' Keith said quietly.

Burton was now desperate. 'Will you pay those cheques?' he pleaded.

Keith looked over the papers on his desk. He stood up. 'Are you absolutely sure that there are no more debts that we should know about?' he demanded.

'Absolutely sure, I promise.'

Keith thought again for a moment. 'Well I *can't* promise,' he said. I'll try to get hold of Mr Telford.'

'And what shall we do about the order?'

'That can wait until tomorrow. The bank's legal department is handling our end of it,' said Keith.

'And what if you can't get hold of Mr Telford?'

Keith shrugged and opened the door for Burton. 'I'll tell you what,' he added, 'if you like, I'll see if I can reach Mr Telford now.'

Burton went out and sat next to the counter toying with the broken chain from which a customer had wrenched the pen. Keith closed the door and went to the telephone. After a delay, he succeeded in putting a call through to Mark. He outlined the conversation and recommended paying Burton's cheque. Mark was slightly hesitant. There might be other bills of which they had no knowledge, but he was prepared to go along with Keith's recommendation and agreed to honour the cheques that were in hand.

Keith put the phone down and opened the door. He went out to the counter and told Burton their decision. Burton was delighted. Keith warned him that there could be no question of a second chance if he was covering anything up. The legal department would sort out the garnishee order, and Burton could return to the problems of bricks and mortar. Burton went away with the air of a man who has been reprieved for a second time.

Keith returned to the office, and sat again in Mark Telford's chair. Carol came in with a stack of papers. He told her to take the cheques for clearing.

'I expect Burton could have kissed you,' she said.

'Yes,' said Keith. 'But he's not my type.'

'Who is then?' said Carol. It was a genuine question.

To her surprise, her complete surprise, she received a genuine answer. 'You,' said Keith.

Carol was amazed.

'I mean it,' said Keith.

'I don't know what to say,' said Carol.

'You could say that you'll come out for a drink with me tonight.'

Carol was now finding it difficult to take Keith seriously. Was this some peculiar result of becoming Manager for the day? She had known that situation to arouse a variety of passions in the hearts of assistant managers, but they were normally more concerned with ambition than romance. 'But you've never . . . I mean so much as . . . '

Keith was as assertive in this conversation, as definite, as he had been with Burton. 'You'd rather I pinched your bottom every time I passed?' he asked.

'You'd have got your shins kicked.'

'There we are then.'

Carol put her hand on her hip. 'Where?' she asked firmly.

'At the King's Head at eight o'clock.'

She allowed four seconds to pass and then said uncertainly, 'All right.'

She began to give Keith her address but he already knew it. She went out looking very surprised.

It was four o'clock when Mark let himself into the house in Islington feeling like an interloper. The house was empty. He went through into the kitchen, idly examined the plants on the window sill and put the kettle on. He realised that he had absolutely nothing to do. He wandered through to the sitting-room and lifted the lid over the keyboard of the piano. He had not the concentration to sit and play properly, but idly fingered a series of notes. From the hall came the unmistakable thump of Peter flinging open the door. Mark played another few notes on the piano and Peter came into the sitting-room.

'Dad, what are you doing home?' he asked.

Peter gave him the headlines on his day.

'Where's Mum?' Peter asked.

'She had an interview this morning. I don't know where she is now,' said Mark.

'Well, she probably got the job and has gone out on the razzle.'

They went through to the kitchen and Mark made tea. Peter asked Mark how he was enjoying Dover, probing gently for any signs that his father's explicable but inconvenient move might be coming to an end. But Mark was definite that he was enjoying himself, that he wasn't bored, and he felt he had made the right decision. Then as he took cups from the cupboard, and with an unusual concession to elegance, saucers as well, Peter asked his father whether he wanted Sylvia to get the job.

'Do you want her to get it?' Mark asked.

'Yes, I do. We could stay in London if she does.'

Mark mused over this for a moment. 'It doesn't affect you really, does it Peter? You'll be off to University and virtually have left home.'

'Hardly,' Peter argued. 'There's the long vacations. And I don't want to come back to a place where I've got no roots and don't know anyone.'

'Of course, but you may not get your "A" levels,' said Mark. 'How's it going?'

'Not bad,' Peter said shrugging.

They were both aware that this conversation was skirting around the real issues. There was a long silence and then Mark said, 'Peter I really want to make a go of that job in Dover. Get to enjoy it.'

'You mean you're not at present?' Peter asked with exactly the expression that Sylvia would have used, a gentle half-smile that implied that the barbed wire is not really sharp.

'No, I don't mean that!' Mark was annoyed at what seemed a deliberate obtuseness in his son.

But Peter went on, 'Who are you trying to convince Dad? Me or you?'

Mark was saved from a reply by the sound of Sylvia coming in through the front door. She was carrying several bags and packages, because she had celebrated her new job with new dresses.

She embraced Mark eagerly. 'Darling! How nice to see you. How long have you been home? Did you come home to celebrate?'

Peter jumped up grinning. 'You got the job then!' he said loudly, with a tone that also implied amazement that his mother might achieve anything at all.

'Yes, I did,' she said, 'I interviewed him and got it.'

Mark looked puzzled. '*You* interviewed *him?*'

'Yes I really did. You wait till I tell you. It was fantastic. Then lunch at Angelo's. Then shopping. What a day! Oh, is that tea there? Great. Just what I need! Tim Hart was marvellous, really . . . civilised.'

'Tim Hart. Didn't he put on that show *Undressed to Kill?*' Mark asked in a voice that expressed great doubts about the level of Tim Hart's civilisation.

Sylvia waved this objection aside. 'Yes, I know, but a commercial management has to make money. It's not subsidised you know. Surely I don't have to convince you that a business must be profitable. He has all sorts of plans for finding new quality plays, and that's where I fit in. He said that with my Arts Council background I probably knew the new writing scene better than he did. I start on Monday, and I have a marvellous office which he says I can decorate how I like, you know, make it cosy . . . Though I don't want to make it like home of course. And over lunch he really convinced me that he did want to find first-class plays. He was very witty about it and compared it to buying a dress. And Mark, wait till you see what I've bought. I've blown all the first month's salary in one afternoon.'

All this came out of Sylvia in one tumbling, excited rush. Mark found himself curiously jealous. It was a long time since he had seen Sylvia so bubbly. What he had failed to do, Tim Hart of *Undressed to Kill*, had achieved in one lunch time. There was a sour note to Mark's voice when he said, 'Oh, he paid you an advance, did he?'

'Don't be so stuffy, Mark,' said Sylvia. 'You don't mind do you?'

'No . . . Now drink that and stop talking while you drink or we'll have to redecorate the kitchen.'

Sylvia sipped her tea and said, more gently, 'Mark it really was good of you to come home. I really do appreciate it.'

'I rang this morning to wish you luck but I was too late. You'd left.'

'I left ridiculously early and had to spend an hour walking around near Shaftesbury Avenue. I was in a right state by the time I got into that interview, believe me.'

Peter had been drinking his tea and looking from one to the other. 'Still you did it,' he said. 'Congratulations. Does it mean we'll get free tickets?'

Sylvia called him a mercenary devil and went upstairs to change. Mark stood silently, staring out of the kitchen window at a rose that was waving gently in the breeze. Peter sat with his cup in his hand, looking at his father.

'Dad, you won't spoil mum's happiness will you?' he asked.

Mark kept his eyes on the rose. 'Why should I do that?'

'Because you don't want her to get a job, at least not in London.'

Mark turned towards his son. 'That's not fair Peter.'

Peter backed down a little. There was still enough of a child in him to submit to the long cool gaze his father was levelling. 'That's good then. I just wanted to say, you know . . . ' His voice tailed away.

'Yes, you said it,' Mark said.

'I'm sorry dad,' Peter said, regaining his strength of will. 'But well, you can spoil things without meaning to.'

Mark walked across to the table, close to Peter's side. 'Does it occur to you that you might be doing that just now,' he asked.

Peter looked up at him. 'A chip off the old block then, eh?' he said.

Later that evening, Carol watched Keith make his way back from the bar with their drinks.

'There we are!' he said, putting them down on the table.

'Thank you . . . cheers.'

They sipped their drinks.

'So . . . tell me about yourself,' Keith said, lounging back in his chair.

Carol looked up, surprised. 'What could I possibly tell you? We've been working together for two years.'

Keith smiled. 'I know that. I mean tell me the secret things.'

'Even more secret than you've found out from reading my file?'

Keith deliberately ignored the sarcasm.

'Oh that's just routine. Name, date of birth, address . . . '

'Ah . . . ' Carol interrupted, 'you want to know the other things. Like – do I live alone, or just simply, "do I"?'

Keith stared at her blankly, a slight flush of crimson creeping up his neck. Carol burst out laughing, unable to hide her amusement. 'You're shocked!'

'No . . . no, of course not.'

'Of course not,' Carol agreed solemnly, 'after all, you're a man of the world.'

'I wouldn't say that . . . '

'You wouldn't need to ask about those sort of things.'

'It wouldn't occur to me,' said Keith, getting further and further into trouble.

'To ask? Or to wonder?' Carol continued, 'or to think of it at all?'

'Well, er . . . I couldn't quite say that.'

Carol laughed again, and he couldn't help wondering why he'd never noticed what a pleasant sound it was.

'Thank God for that anyway . . . '

Somehow he realised they'd come to the end of round one, the first faltering steps of their relationship were now taken.

'I have the distinct impression that I haven't started very well at all,' he observed ironically before he went to the bar for some more drinks.

When he came back, they chatted about their respective careers at the Bank and eventually got round to the subject of Mark Telford.

'He *is* a very attractive man. Every inch a manager.' Carol enthused.

Keith agreed, but couldn't understand why such a man should choose to leave the International Division to become a local branch manager. 'I expect you find it romantic,' he said to Carol, 'giving up everything for the simple life.'

'Actually, I find it a bit wet,' Carol retorted. 'If I get to be an International Manager I'd be damned if you'd find me asking to come back to somewhere like Dover.'

Keith looked up, as though the idea of Carol wanting a career had never occurred to him. 'You plan to get on do you?' he asked her.

'Yes . . . that is, as long as you approve.'

Keith realised, too late, they were verging on dangerous ground again.

'Are you going to try to put me down all evening?'

'What do you mean?' Carol looked as though she'd regretted her quick reply.

'Listen. I don't trust the sort of woman who wants to be liberated just to be free to cut off a man's balls.'

Carol had begun to look hurt.

'Do you think I'm like that?' she asked.

'Not really,' Keith relented, 'but I'd say you'd established a *primae facie* case.'

'I'm sorry. Looks like I haven't started very well either.'

Keith warmed to her quickly. 'Well, I think we've established we've both got teeth so let's go and eat shall we? And we can start again.'

Pleased to have her family around her, and spurred on by the events of the day, Sylvia produced a magnificent supper for the three of them.

Peter was particularly appreciative. He also revealed a startling knowledge of garnishee orders.

'It's a high court order served on a man who owes money to someone by someone else,' he explained to his mother, 'who is owed money by that man . . . saying that he mustn't pay back the money to the man who is owed money . . . by the man who is the subject of the order . . . if you see what I mean.'

Mark was very surprised. 'He's right,' he said. 'Technically it is the order served on a creditor of a judgement debtor by a judgement creditor. But how on earth did you know, Peter? I didn't even know that this morning. My assistant had to explain it to me.'

Peter revealed that it was a pure fluke. He had been skimming through a commercial dictionary when he had come across the word, which had taken his fancy.

'Is it very serious?' Sylvia asked.

'Not for us,' Mark explained. 'Bit of a nuisance, that's all. Waste of money for the creditor too. The chap owes us thousands, so there's nothing to seize. Our legal men will go to the court and say the cupboard's bare, and that's that. My customer gets his knuckles rapped of course, for not telling us of the judgement debt, and on we go, each of us hoping against hope that he'll pull us out of the mire and be able to pay us both off.'

Mark was describing this with as much moral concern as he would have granted to a verbatim account of a Third Division football match. But Sylvia saw the human aspect. 'Poor chap,' she said, sadly.

Peter excused himself and went off to get his guitar, as he was off to meet the group for rehearsal.

After he had gone Mark said, 'He doesn't do enough work.'

Sylvia left the table. 'Would you like to see my new dress?' she asked.

'Yes, I'd love to.'

She collected some of the plates and glasses from the table and put them in the kitchen before going upstairs to change. Mark tidied the rest away after her and went into the sitting-room to the piano. He raised the lid, sat on the stool and stood selecting in his mind the music that would be most appropriate. It was one of those evenings when his conscious mind absented itself as he played. The music flowed from him as though he were inventing it, all the lights and shades coming easily to his fingers.

Sylvia came quietly into the room and stood listening to the music. It was a long time since she had heard Mark play like this. At these moments she realised what a complicated man Mark was, for all his apparent single-mindedness, and why she loved him.

He looked up from the piano and saw her. She was wearing a simple but effective black dress with white trimmings. He took the music to the end of a phrase and then stopped. 'Oh very nice,' he said. 'I like it. I like it very much.'

Sylvia looked back at him. 'Good,' she said, and after a pause: 'You're not very happy are you?'

Mark smiled over the piano. 'I'm fine,' he said. He began to play another phrase of the Chopin quietly.

Sylvia took a few steps into the room. 'You're angry about my job,' she said.

'No. Absolutely not,' said Mark.

Sylvia wasn't making herself clear. 'I don't mean *angry* . . . more disappointed or . . . worried about it . . . '

This was precisely what Mark had hoped to avoid. He was being forced to articulate things which he would have preferred to have lost in the Chopin. 'It's not as simple as that, Sylvia. This is your day and I don't want to spoil it . . . '

Sylvia took another step towards him. 'It's no good playing games of "let's pretend everything in the garden's lovely." '

Mark searched for words that would convey the confusions in his spirit. 'It's just that we're both in a transition . . . we're both moving . . . but in opposite directions . . . '

She came to the piano and rested her hand on the walnut wood. 'It *is* my job isn't it!'

'No!' Mark said immediately. 'Not in isolation. If I'd still been in the International Division it would have been an excellent idea.'

Sylvia's voice softened. 'Are you sorry you gave that up?'

'No! At lunch today we were talking about retirement. It's not so far away and it's not worrying about what I'll do when I retire, that's not it. It's just that thinking about retirement puts a different perspective on your life *now*. I'm not saying that work isn't important. It is. It's very important to me, but there do have to be other things, other relationships.'

Sylvia thought about it. 'You mean if you didn't have to retire, you *could* make your work your whole life.'

'You could. Whether it would be a good idea is another thing altogether.'

Sylvia nodded agreement. 'It makes sense. You ought to have other things in your life apart from work.'

Mark was speaking now with a quiet seriousness, saying things that he had not articulated to himself before. 'Well,

I suddenly realised I had nothing else. Work was absolutely challenging but it was all there was. I was losing you and Peter. I was paying too high a price for the stimulation of work. A work-junkie. The mind keeps on a high because of the continual shots, but the rest of the body declines by malnutrition and neglect.'

'So you've put yourself on a sensible bland diet to build yourself up again,' Sylvia said. 'But Mark I've been on that bland diet for years and I'm bored stiff with it.'

'I've realised that. That was one of the reasons for the change, to broaden our lives together, to use the boat more, to . . . well, to see each other occasionally I suppose.'

Sylvia shook her head. 'It's not enough Mark. I'm not here just to change my function in response to you. I have my own life too.'

'I realise that,' Mark said.

If they had been skirting around the subject before, moving away from it on every occasion that it presented itself, there would be no avoiding it now. Sylvia leaned a little nearer to Mark, her hands on the lid of the piano.

'Do you? Do you really?' she demanded. 'We've been married what, nineteen years? We've built up this home, brought up Peter. But that's been *my* life, not yours, and I've done it, it's finished. I can't just go on deciding to change the colour of the curtains or thinking of an endless line of dinners to cook. You were worrying about retiring in fifteen years time, but I've retired *now*. I've done my job and I want another. Don't keep saying you understand me. Because you don't, you've never even tried. You changed your job because you felt your needs have changed. Fair enough. Well, now I've done the same. You simply moved first.'

Mark was becoming angry. He was stung by the truth in what Sylvia was saying, but he could not accept it completely. There were factors about his life, their lives, that Sylvia was not taking into account. 'Damn it all!' he said. 'I won't be cast a villain in your private play, I'm *not* a possessive husband, terrified of every step you take outside the home! Let's put the cards on the table. Do you think it was a mistake for me to give in the international job?'

Sylvia took her hands off the piano and turned slightly

away. 'It's not for me to judge.'

'It is if I ask you!'

'You're asking too much. I have to trust that you know what's best for yourself. If you insist, I must say that I think you made a mistake.'

There was a long silence and then Mark said. 'I see.' There was another longer pause before he added, 'It would obviously be much more convenient if I did spend most of the time away from home.'

Sylvia's frustration was now transmitted into a dull anger. 'That isn't worthy of you Mark,' she said.

'I'm sorry,' Mark repeated. 'But everyone insists in seeing my movements as a retreat. It's not. It's just a change.'

Sylvia seemed to visibly brace herself for what she was about to say. 'That's fine,' she said quietly. 'If you're completely happy about it, what does it matter what everyone else thinks?'

He stood looking at her standing there in her new dress, her hair still neatly arranged. In the dim, rosy light from the standard lamp, he could just discern the thin track of a tear on her cheek. Slowly he dropped his eyes to the keyboard, not wanting her to see the quiet desperation that filled his eyes too. He held his fingers over the keyboard a moment before he began to play a long, sad phrase of Schubert.

He lifted his eyes to meet hers, but continued playing, and smiled wanly. 'I can't resist feeling that I served a garnishee order on our joint account,' he said quietly. 'But it was overdrawn.'

Sylvia did not reply. She walked slowly round behind him, and stood there for a moment, putting her hands on his shoulders. Their words were exhausted. Nothing else they could say at that moment would add any comfort. Their lives, which had once been so closely related were now drawing apart against both their wishes.

Mark was still playing an hour after Sylvia had silently left the room.

Chapter Five

A month passed. During this time Mark had settled into his chair in the Dover branch of Knight's Bank. He felt now that he understood the business, and a great many of the personal patterns of the town. Sylvia and Peter seemed to accept the situation, though Mark still found his evenings lonely and wished that Sylvia would join him in the cottage. During their meetings she recounted to him the ups and downs of the London theatre scene, and Mark felt a slight pang of jealousy for that speculative world where profit margins swelled or shrunk according to intangibles ranging from the reviews in the Sundays and 'Time Out', to the whims of an uncertain public. If he was honest with himself, much as he enjoyed the day to day business in the bank, it was pedestrian compared to the life that Sylvia was apparently leading.

For her part Sylvia had become resigned to the division between her and Mark and found she adjusted quickly to the new rhythms of her existence. She revelled in the theatre world, and as she became better and more expert in her job, so the enjoyment of that increased. Tim Hart was witty, amusing, serious, business-like, and given to unexpected gestures that made life sufficiently secure for her not to worry in her work but sufficiently variable for her to have experienced not a moment of boredom.

Peter had divided his life into three. The smallest part he devoted to school work. He was intelligent and had inherited his father's capacity for rapid judgement. He found that he could assimilate his 'A' level text books without any vast exertion. Unlike his father, however, he could see no point in expending energy needlessly. He was a typical member of a generation led by the media to believe that energy of any form was a precious resource which could be given up only at some cost to the planet. The second, and slightly larger, part of his life he gave to Jenny. Slowly, she was liberating those parts of her soul, or more interestingly her body, which previously she had kept to herself. Whenever they talked, much of the conversation was dominated by the unusual lives his parents were leading. Jenny was his only confidante. If she resented his preoccupation with the domestic peculiarities of the Telfords she made no complaint. She was aware of her importance as a sounding-board for his fluctuating opinions, and sensitive enough to realise that without her he might express his confusion in less direct ways. It gave her, too, a sense of herself as a woman, even though she could offer no real advice to Peter.

The third and largest portion of his life was given up to music; endless practice on his quieter evenings, devoted solely to listening carefully to the music of groups he admired and then trying to capture all his ideas when the band played together.

Keith and Carol had spent nearly every evening since their first date drinking in pubs in and around Dover. They had consumed enough alcohol to earn themselves a special commendation from the brewery, and it was a toss-up whether they would reach a more private and less alcoholic phase of their relationship before inflicting serious kidney damage on themselves. They found over the weeks that they had more and more to say to each other.

The cliffs provided them with many a pleasant evening walk, but the scenery faded over the weeks like an old instant photograph of beach and sky. In the bank they were restrained. If anything they were more formal and courteous to each other than they had been before Keith's unexpected and bold invitation for Carol to join him for a drink. They were both ambitious professionals and, within the confines of the bank, if either of them had made a move which might predispose Mark Telford to think badly of them, the intimacy would have evaporated as swiftly as the bubbles in warm tonic water.

If Mark Telford could have foreseen, as he sat reading the *Financial Times* on the London to Dover train, on a Monday morning, the results that would flow from a casual meeting, he might have walked to Dover. But instead, he became aware that a young man was standing in the aisle of the train next to him and looked up. He was tall and broad shouldered, with his fair hair short and neatly cut. He introduced himself as Christopher Maddox. His father was the owner of Maddox Engineering. Mark remembered his meeting with Maddox when he had been doing his first rounds of the town with Tom Stetchley. He motioned to the seat opposite him and Christopher Maddox sat down.

Maddox had been up to London for a 'bit of a party', and was going straight to his office, where, he told Mark, he kept a suit. His father was a stickler for neatness and punctuality, especially by the family. The purpose of his chat with Mark was not all social pleasantness. A friend of his was selling a Jaguar XJ6 for the modest sum of four thousand pounds and Maddox wondered whether his friendly Bank Manager might be willing to float a little loan before this miraculous bargain was snapped up by someone else. Mark asked whether he had a company car. Indeed he had, but his father had insisted on it being a Cortina and that was hardly the sort of car to provide the best image for the younger Maddox to roar about the highways and byways of Kent.

When Christopher Maddox suggested the way in which they might arrange the loan, Mark brought the conversation to a halt. He pointed out that the Consumer Credit Act of 1974, implied that, theoretically, whatever arrangement they came to in the train could later be denied by Christopher Maddox and the bank could lose all its money. But of course, if Christopher Maddox would like to ring and arrange an appointment at the Bank, they could look at all the details that might be involved in a personal loan. Maddox said he certainly would be in touch very soon, and as the train was approaching Dover he excused himself and went off to fetch his overnight bag.

When he had been through the routine Monday morning paperwork with Carol, Mark asked to see all the Maddox files, including the personal files and particularly Christopher's account. It took only a glance to see that he was overdrawn.

Keith turned out to know all about the young Maddox, even though as he explained to Mark, Maddox wasn't exactly his cup of tea. He had been at school with him. Not terribly bright, not like his younger brother. Very good at rugger, had a reputation for treating girls badly, and was not, in Keith's view, a very likeable personality. But if he wanted to borrow four thousand pounds for a Jaguar, it would be good business for the bank. Even if they didn't take a guarantee from his father, the old man could hardly afford to let his own son default.

'No,' said Mark, 'that's true. But the father's account is more important. If he makes an application, we'd insist on a guarantee. It's a way of letting his father know before we incur his wrath by lending his son four thousand.'

Keith agreed that this was a good idea. Mark looked over the firm's figures and asked Keith what he thought of them. Keith did not think they were very good but in his view there was nothing serious to worry about. Mark was not convinced. He examined the accounts more closely.

'Seven years ago,' he said, 'the gross profit was a hundred and fourteen thousand pounds, with a fall the next year to eighty thousand pounds, then a plateau for the next three years at about the eighty thousand mark, finally a gross profit last year of sixty thousand. It's a text book case. Maddox's father started the firm, didn't he?'

'Yes. He was a grand old chap, tough as old nails. Died about nine years ago.'

Mark looked up from the paper. 'Well, you know the old saying. "Clogs to clogs in three generations." '

Keith was puzzled. Did Mark really think the firm could fail suddenly?

'No; there's too much fat on it. But if young Christopher gets his hands on it . . . '

'Yes,' said Keith. 'Of course, Mr Stetchley was always trying to make them get in some new blood to expand and diversify a bit.'

Mark certainly agreed with his predecessor's judgement. 'That's what he'll have to do if the firm is to survive his son. Perhaps I should give it a go. It's time I gave my golf balls an airing.'

The fairway of the third hole stretched away from the tee under a sky of grey and white. Mark had not approached the top few rungs of the ladder of Knight's Bank without cultivating a rather good drive. The ball sizzled in a curving arc and bounced down the centre just short of the green. Maddox nodded his appreciation. As he was teeing up his ball, Mark said, 'By the way, I met your son the other day.'

'Let's leave talking about my son until I've hit this ball,' said Maddox. 'You can tell Tom Stetchley trained you. He always used to say nothing till the third tee and then bring up the business. If I got to the fourth without him saying anything I knew I could enjoy the game. Always picked up from then on.'

'Oh, let's leave it then,' said Mark. Maddox made no reply but addressed the ball and sent it to rest parallel with the green but off to one side in the rough.

'My son wanted a loan for four thousand pounds for a Jag,' said Maddox. 'You told him that you needed my guarantee, but you knew I wouldn't let him default.'

'It just seemed prudent banking,' said Mark as they walked down the trim grass.

'Rubbish! It was a way of letting me know,' said Maddox. Mark walked ten or fifteen yards before replying. 'It does have that effect . . . I wouldn't want to cause any disruption in our relationship . . . or in your family if it comes to that.'

Maddox graced Mark with one of his rare smiles. 'I'm grateful. Christopher has changed his mind about wanting the loan.'

'Oh, I'm sure that's wise,' said Mark.

'So am I,' said Maddox.

Their paths diverged as Maddox went off into the long grass to make a very neat chip from the rough to a point some eight inches from the hole. Mark grinned and selected his iron for the contest.

At the sixth tee, after a perfect drive, Maddox himself returned to the subject of business. He had a feeling that Christopher's loan was not the real reason for this game, because Mark had arranged it before Christopher had been into the bank to arrange his loan in the right setting.

Mark paused with his golf club in his hand. He ran his fingers over the smooth wooden butt and balanced the weight of it across his hand. 'All right,' he said. 'I give your business ten years.'

Maddox's mouth dropped open in amazement. 'That's rubbish!' he said.

Mark addressed the ball, paused and went on: 'I hope so, but I believe not. You're vulnerable in two ways, one immediate and one in the long-term.' He gave the ball a vicious blow, smoothed down the divot and gestured down the fairway before continuing. 'The immediate threat is a takeover bid. I've never seen such a vulnerable company. It's a sitting duck. I can't understand why nobody's tried before now.'

'Because the family controls the shares. We're fireproof,' he said, striding confidently out ahead of Mark.

'You own twenty-one percent. Your sons own ten percent each. Your uncle has ten percent, also in trust for your sons. That makes fifty-one percent and effective control. Your yield is lowered because you don't employ your capital as well as you might. Even so, your market price was a hundred and forty-eight on Friday.' Mark walked along a few paces behind Maddox.

'I don't watch the figures every day,' said Maddox, half turning and allowing Mark to catch him up.

'Which makes the company worth almost three hundred thousand pounds,' Mark went on. 'But a bidder can offer a premium, and bearing in mind the under-used, wasting assets – it would be a big one, making the company worth what – half a million?'

Maddox waved his hand dismissively. He stopped to

watch a flock of migrating swallows ride across the sky and behind the tree line before saying, 'It's all just figures. If we control the shares they could offer the moon. It doesn't matter.'

Mark frowned. 'At half a million, Christopher's ten percent would be worth fifty thousand pounds, and after your uncle dies he gets an extra five percent from his trust – how old is your uncle anyway?"

'Eighty-two.'

'Mm . . . interesting. Well after that, Christopher's share would be seventy-five thousand pounds, or 18.75 Jaguars.'

Maddox stopped. He could plainly be an aggressive man and he was aggressive now. 'Are you saying . . . '

'I'm not saying anything specific Mr Maddox,' Mark went on immediately. 'As you were saying, it's all just figures.'

'Christopher wouldn't sell his shares.' The big man strode off again towards his perfectly-placed ball.

'Then you've absolutely nothing to worry about on that score. Good.'

Maddox stopped and his golfing bag swung on his shoulder with the sudden stop. 'I'll give you this hole, Telford,' he said. 'All right, you've succeeded in rattling me. Which means you're a better man than Tom was. You think we ought to have a proper meeting, really thrash everything out?'

'If that's what you want,' said Mark. 'We're at your disposal.'

Mark wished he had a photographic memory for his diary at least, but when Maddox suggested Tuesday at ten o'clock he agreed without hesitation.

Maddox nodded firmly, in a way that completely terminated that subject of conversation. 'Now,' he said briskly. 'Where's the bloody seventh tee!'

He walked off towards it leaving Mark to follow.

On Tuesday, the grey cloud darkened and it began to drizzle. But Maddox was not interested in discussing the weather as he sat in Mark's office.

'Let's not beat around the bush, Telford,' he said. 'I want to get on with it.'

'As you wish,' said Mark. 'You want me to tell you why your business is in danger from under-investment.'

'No.'

'I'm sorry . . . '

Maddox was a man who liked to say what there was to be said and get it over with, and he preferred other people to be the same. 'You said on Sunday that my business is in danger from a takeover bid.'

Mark nodded. 'Yes, that's true, but the two things are not unconnected, you know.'

'Rubbish! Really Telford, the two things are quite separate.'

Mark settled himself comfortably in his chair before continuing. 'Well, I'll tell you what I think, then it's up to you. The question to ask is, why are companies taken over? I suppose there are two main reasons, firstly the business would fit neatly into the bidder's business, making up a gap in their product range, or increasing their production or diversifying their interest in the market. Anything like that. Those are, we could say *production reasons.*'

'Secondly there is the type where it's not the product which is of primary interest to the bidder. He has financial reasons for wanting to buy the business.'

'Asset strippers!' Maddox interrupted disdainfully.

'Well maybe,' Mark went on, 'but not necessarily. Perhaps he wants to broaden his financial base, increase his capital, all sorts of things. But it's true that he will hope to restructure the business to release some assets – maybe to sell, maybe to use productively, but this will give him good financial reasons to make a bid. So let's not quarrel about words. The point is, the *real point* is, that for both types a company that is running below par is particularly attractive . . . '

There was a loud sniff from Maddox. 'And who defines what's a *"par"*?'

'Oh, that's easy,' Mark replied. 'It's what you could be doing with what you have. If you are doing less than you could, you have, in fact, got capital tied up. It's just like having thousands of pounds hidden in your mattress instead of earning interest for you in a bank, or a building society. Now the price of a company is what it is doing. Not what it *could* be doing. If a bid is successful the bidder buys the mattress for the cost of the mattress and all the pound notes he gets for nothing.

'So, even if the bidder is completely straight, interested only in production, it makes more sense for him to buy your company, because it is cheaper for him that way, rather than by setting up in competition, having to buy all new factories and so on . . . '

Maddox interrupted again. 'Yes I see all that . . . But it still supposes that the bidder *can* buy enough shares. I mean if you've got fifty-one percent locked up, the bid can't succeed.'

Mark agreed. 'No, of course not. As far as the bid is concerned the position changes from being a dangerous one to being a useless one.'

Maddox was obviously learning to like Mark Telford, despite his criticisms of the company. The heavy man smiled, begrudgingly, and said, 'You don't mess about, do you Telford? Pull any punches?'

'Would you like it better if I did?' Mark said, knowing the answer.

'No. So in my situation you try to make sure that the shares don't get out?'

That wasn't good enough for Mark. 'That's very negative,' he said. 'I'd advise you to make your company so efficient that it would be too expensive to buy to make it worthwhile for anyone to try.'

Maddox was prepared at least to listen to this. 'Maybe you're right.' he said. 'Oh, by the way, while I remember it, I had a chat with Chris last night – I was probably too hard on him – I've decided to guarantee that loan for the car. Damn it, one's only young once . . . '

Mark wasn't prepared to expend much energy on the question of Christopher's Jaguar at the moment. He muttered something about the securities clerk drawing up a guarantee. And then said, returning to the more pressing matter of Maddox's company, that he would like to go over the books in great detail, and see the factories, the land, the property and all the assets. Depending on what he found, he might need to take some advice.

Maddox could not go against a man as business-like as Mark. 'All right,' he said. 'When do we start?'

'How about tomorrow? I could come up to your factory tomorrow morning.'

Maddox nodded. 'Right. I get there at eight. Give me half an hour to look at the mail.'

There was unmistakable horror in Mark's voice as he exclaimed, 'Half past eight!'

Maddox smiled. 'Too early for you?'

Mark was not to be outdone by this, though it was a remarkably early hour for him to be poring over books, trudging through factories. 'Not at all,' he said. 'I'll see you at half past eight.'

Maddox stood up and Mark made his way towards the door, but there was plainly something else on Maddox's mind. He held back for a moment.

'Oh, there's one more thing,' he added. 'A bit of a nerve really. You were saying on Sunday that your chief relaxation was playing the piano?'

'Yes?' said Mark tentatively.

'Well I'm the president of the Gilbert and Sullivan Society, I roar away in the chorus as well. We're doing "Mikado" this year, just started. Well our pianist has got the flu. Damn nuisance . . . It's a hell of a cheek I know, but I wondered if you would mind helping us out this evening. It's the first chorus rehearsal you see.'

Mark's mind ran through six possible excuses, none of them good enough.

'Well, I've never done anything like that before,' he said.

'I know it's a cheek,' said Maddox, with a tone that suggested that cheek was perfectly excusable. 'But I would be grateful.'

Mark accepted that he had no alternative and agreed to be at the Church at half past seven that evening.

Mark would have preferred to have spent the evening studying the files of Maddox's accounts. Instead he found himself in a crowded church hall, making polite small talk, and preparing himself to accompany the budding Mikados and Nanky Poos of Dover. The Reverend Kenton introduced him with embarrassing play on the words 'note' and 'notes' and hoped that the Gilbert and Sullivan Society would not exploit this opportunity to take their revenge on the Bank Manager. Despite his apparent assurance, Mark was not at all comfortable on these occasions. He did not like being the focus of the attention of a large crowd of people. He certainly was prone to moments of acting in his private life or over a luncheon table, but he had no urge to join this merry band, even in rehearsal, and would positively have refused to play for the performance.

But as the evening progressed, and he was no longer the star turn but merely the accompanist, he found he could sight-read the music without too much difficulty, and busk his way through the rest, so that there was almost enjoyment in the activity. The conductor was kind, the chorus was acceptably tuneful, and he was a little sorry when the rehearsal broke up for the evening.

Maddox went directly to him as Mark stood and shut the lid on the piano. The hall was echoing with the chatter of the choir, as rehearsal began to adopt its other function, a chance for social meetings and gossip. Maddox was surprised and delighted by Mark's pianistic achievements. He even went so far as to say that he hoped that their regular pianist had a long convalescence. Mark muttered something deflating about pressure of work and unpredictable movements, but the Reverend Kenton, who was now by their sides, insisted that they must make a firm date with him for the following Monday.

'After all,' the Vicar said pointedly, 'it's as good a way as any for getting to know the people in town, and as a matter of fact half the Parish Council are in the chorus.'

Mark took the point and grinned. 'Now you wouldn't be trying to blackmail me, would you Vicar?'

'I am sure a bank manager is as incorruptible as a Vicar...'

Mark agreed to play for them the following Monday, but he would not go and join the company in the pub. He pointed to his briefcase and said, 'I'm up early in the morning, and that briefcase is full of your files . . . to be read tonight. And I'm sure you would be very hard on anyone who hadn't done his homework Mr Maddox.'

In Islington, Peter and Sylvia were speculating about Mark's progress with the Gilbert and Sullivan Society. Mark had telephoned her at the office to pass on his exciting news that he would be compèring his way through the evening and when she told Peter, he had laughed uproariously. 'He can't dish it out all the time,' said Peter. 'He has to take it occasionally.'

Sylvia frowned. 'Do you think he does – always dish it out?'

'Well, yes, he does. He has a sort of unnerving confidence. Makes him very hard to argue with. You *feel* he knows what he's talking about, even if he doesn't.'

'His professional skill,' said Sylvia.

Peter nodded. 'I suppose so,' he said, and resorted again to giggles at the thought of his father locked in the church hall with the old ladies of Dover.

'But you don't find it really difficult to talk to him do you?' asked Sylvia.

Peter sobered up and considered this. 'Depends about what. I would rather talk to you about me and I'd rather talk to dad about the world – sometimes he seems to want to get close and then something stops him.'

Sylvia found herself more and more surprised at the acute perceptions of her son. It was hard to accept that he was changing and maturing, because when she looked at him he was part of a continuum stretching back over seventeen years. 'I'm sure most people would be surprised to know just how shy he really is. He is happiest facing a problem that is reduced to a balance sheet,' she observed.

This worried Peter. 'Sounds very . . . *cold*,' he said.

Sylvia shook her head. 'The reverse, in fact. He feels *too* much. It hurts. It's just self-defence.'

The sounds in the foundry were deafening. Metal clashed on metal, and scrap iron tumbled on metal sheets with screeching and rumbling that echoed through the bare roofs; molten metal cascaded, hissing violently, and spitting lethal droplets as it filled the moulds made in the shape of the special valves that Maddox's father had developed.

Maddox said that they had few industrial troubles. Only half the men were in the union and were prepared to work as much for loyalty as for wages. Mark wondered how long that state of affairs would last, but refrained from commenting.

The storerooms of the foundry were stacked to the ceilings with supplies. Maddox had laid in enough to withstand a year's coal-strike, steel strike, and electricity strike. He was proud of his foresight.

In the machine shop they watched the castings being turned, polished, and assembled. Half of the space in this large shed was empty.

'What's that area down there?' Mark asked.

'Nothing,' said Maddox. 'I suppose you want to stuff it full of machines?'

'Well, you are paying rates for the space,' said Mark.

Maddox paused for a moment and asked one of the workers how his wife was getting along since getting out of hospital, and then led Mark up to the office block. It was part of the original buildings of the factory, most of the windows were smashed and dirty and Mark wondered whether the factory inspectors would consider the lighting adequate. Maddox dismissed them as 'those buggers'. Hunched over a desk in the twilight of a small office was an ancient Dickensian figure sorting invoices. Mr Templar, Maddox explained, had been with the firm since it started, as a messenger boy with his father.

It was a quick but comprehensive tour. Mark had seen everything that he needed to see, but he still had many questions to ask Maddox. They sat in his office, and sipped hot coffee. Mark began his analysis.

'Looking at your balance sheet,' he said, 'it seems to me that seventy per cent of your turnover comes from that valve assembly.'

Maddox nodded. 'As a matter of fact we're the biggest suppliers, forty-five per cent of the market,' he said

'And the market is the gas industry,' Mark went on. 'No one else buys it.'

None of this was news to Maddox. 'No,' he said, 'it's specially designed to fit gas mains.'

Mark looked up at the ceiling. 'I see; so if someone invented a cheaper system you would go bust overnight?'

Maddox had thought of this, but it really was not a possibility that he would consider. The system had been tried and tested over the years, and there was no way of making it cheaper.

'That's what boat builders used to say about wood,' said Mark pointedly. 'Did you think of trying to adapt it for the oil industry in the North Sea?'

Maddox explained that the pressures were different, but he agreed that they should have chased up that idea. It might not be too late. Oil pipe lines were being laid continuously.

'Well, there's a start,' said Mark. 'You need a research and development department . . . '

This was a return to a psalm that Tom Stetchley had sung continuously to Maddox's irritation. He expected something better than this from Mark.

'Oh, dear,' he said.

'I know,' Mark went on, 'But you can pay for it with that ridiculous expense of carrying all that stock. It's not good to have such a high proportion of your turnover resting on such a comparatively simple product. You've got to diversify, find some new products.'

Maddox had heard enough of this. 'What else?' he demanded.

Mark refused to be hurried. 'Look, would you let me have a few hours going over your stock system for a start. Mr Templar can give me what I want. I don't want to take up your time. I'll take some stuff back up to the Bank, and work on it. We'll meet again on Wednesday.'

Maddox nodded.

* * *

Christopher Maddox was completing his Loan Application Form with Keith's assistance. He signed it and pushed it back across the desk.

'Right,' said Keith. 'Well, as soon as Mr Telford gets back with the guarantee form completed you will have four thousand pounds credited to you.'

'Excellent!' Christopher Maddox said in the drawling manner that Keith had found so irritating at school, and found no better now. 'Thank you very much.'

But Keith was too good a professional to let his distaste

show. 'Not at all. If your father guarantees the loan, it's very good business for us.'

Christopher Maddox smiled. 'Oh yes. He'll guarantee it. I mean I own ten per cent of the firm, don't I, and we have to stick together to keep control. My father wouldn't want me to upset him at this time, would he?'

Keith was prevented by replying by Mark's arrival back at the office from the foundry. He had brought the guarantee form with him, signed and completed by Christopher Maddox's father.

'Good'o!' said Christopher. 'Well, I'll be off to see a man about a Jag.'

When he had shut the door behind him, Mark said, 'That young man does not improve on knowing him better.'

'No!' Keith said emphatically. 'He seems to positively enjoy his ten per cent over his father.'

Mark Telford grimaced, 'Yes . . . '

Keith looked at his watch and pointed out that it was nearly closing time. But before he could go Mark said, 'What do you mean he seems to enjoy his ten per-cent hold over his father? What did he say exactly?'

Keith thought for a moment, 'Something about, "having to keep together to keep control . . . and . . . his father not wanting to upset him at this time . . . " '

Mark leaned on the edge of the desk, looking puzzled. 'That's strange,' he said. 'I'm sure Maddox wouldn't spell it out to his son. It's not his style . . . Strange . . . Where's the Financial Times?'

Keith passed it across the desk. Mark shuffled through the pages until he came to the list of share prices. He ran his finger down the column until he found the right place.

'Maddox . . . Maddox . . . Here we are . . . one hundred and fifty-two . . . That's four points up since Friday, and they went up three last week. The F.T. Industrial Index is down five points, but Maddox is up four.' He put the paper down and looked across at Keith. 'I wonder who's buying Maddox's shares?'

Chapter Six

The next morning, Maddox Engineering was up another two points to 154. *Somebody* was buying, and since it was unlikely that they were buying merely to have shares in a lethargic family engineering works, there was a strong possibility that a takeover bid was in the offing.

Maddox would have none of it when Mark phoned him. He took it merely as an indication that somebody had confidence in the old firm. He had not inspected the share register because old Templar looked after that. And in any case he wondered why Mark was sufficiently panicked to make an early phone call to him when he was coming up to the plant at half-past nine anyway. After a cursory good-bye, Mark put the telephone down sharply and sat looking at it for a moment. He looked across at Keith Everly, who raised his eyebrows. 'I'm going to try and talk him into getting in our Merchant Banking boys straight away,' said Mark. 'If there is going to be a fight the sooner they're briefed the better.'

Casting a play is like fitting together a jigsaw puzzle with only half the pieces. Actors who are available in theory from a certain date are suddenly offered roles in television plays or feature films, and have to be removed from the cast. Sylvia was having a hard time that morning with an agent whose actors and actresses appeared to be perpetually on the brink of other work and incapable of deciding anything until all other possibilities had been turned down.

Tim Hart stood in the doorway of her office and watched her as she talked on the phone. When she put it back in its cradle for a moment he said, 'Your husband must be a lunatic . . . going away and leaving a lovely lady like you.'

Sylvia gave him one of those 'oh-come-on-you'll-have-to-do-better-than-that' looks. 'And what do I say to that . . . "Oh, sir this is so sudden. I never knew you cared"?'

Tim cocked his head in an exaggerated performance of deep thought. 'Not bad. But maybe . . . "My husband and I have never cared for each other, and now he's gone I feel a tremendous relief" might be better." ' Although he said this with a smile, it was not an altogether casual remark.

'Ah, well. I'm afraid not,' Sylvia said. 'In this management we only deal in truthful plays.'

Tim staggered into the room like a man in the grip of coronary thrombosis. 'What!' he cried. 'My God, you'll bankrupt me!'

Sylvia laughed. 'I'll certainly do that if you don't let me get on casting this play.'

Tim sobered up. 'Don't worry, I won't stop the good work. This came in today.'

He handed her a letter, and as she read through it he said, 'It's from Newcastle . . . new play. Don't know the writer, but I do know the Director. He recommends it. I think we should take a look at it.'

'Newcastle!' said Sylvia, making it sound as though he had suggested a quick trip to Timbuctoo.

'Yes,' he said. 'There's a lot of England north of Watford, you know.'

'Really,' Sylvia said in her strongest Scots accent. 'There's a lot of Britain north of Newcastle, too.'

Tim Hart clutched his forehead in precisely the histrionic manner that would have enraged him if one of his actors had dared to try it.

'Oh my God! This isn't my day is it? Look, let's pretend I've just come in and I'll start again. Do you think you could go to Newcastle one day this week?'

'You want me to go alone?' Sylvia asked.

'If you insist,' Tim said in a very sexy voice, the sound of a man whose deep passions have been frustrated.

'Tim!' Sylvia reproved him.

'Yes!' he half-shouted. 'Alone!'

Sylvia considered it for a moment. 'How about Thursday? Peter could stay over with one of his friends.'

Tim nodded. The matter was settled. 'Fine. I'm going up to Manchester to see another play that night. I'll get Pat to fix up a hotel for you.'

As he went through the stock sheets with the aged Mr Templar, Mark was amazed at the volume of stock that Maddox was holding. If the factory had been an ark, then Noah Maddox could have survived many a flood. When they had finished the analysis, Mark coaxed a few memories from Mr Templar. His knowledge of the firm was encyclopaedic.

'Most of the capital was subscribed in old Mr Maddox's time,' said Templar. 'Lots of local people bought shares, you know, and they've hung on to them. Sound investment. As a matter of fact one share transfer form came in this morning.'

Mark tried not to be too eager, 'Oh, who's buying the shares?'

'I really don't know,' said Templar. 'I haven't entered it yet.'

His desk was piled high with invoices, bills, receipts, notes from the local council on amendments to Planning Acts, and Templar scrabbled through these for a moment or to before coming up with the transfer paper. At Mark's request he passed it over, and Mark looked at it carefully, frowning.

'Thank you,' he said. 'I'll just have a word with Mr Maddox before I go, and thank you for all your help, Mr Templar.'

In Maddox's office, Mark came straight to the point. 'Why are you buying you're own shares?'

'Why not?' demanded Maddox. 'I've got faith in the firm. Nothing illegal about it, is there?'

Mark had to admit that there was nothing illegal about it, but he did not consider it a wise move. Maddox snorted. Mark Telford was continually threatening him with a takeover bid. Obviously the more shares he held the safer he was.

'But you're drawing attention to yourself,' Mark said. 'Look, I rang you this morning to ask you who was buying your shares. Do you think I'm the only person in England who reads the share prices?'

Mark had a valid point.

'Mmm,' said Maddox. 'Well, I must say I didn't expect the price to rise like that.'

'Well if you'd have asked I would have told you. The fact is, there's very little trading in your shares. If you order, say, five thousand of them, the jobber almost certainly hasn't got any to sell. He has to put the price up to try to make a market. And in any case you can hardly affect the issue. You have one thousand three hundred shares issued. And they're selling today at one fifty-four. So if you spend five thousand pounds, you can hardly raise your holding by one per cent!' This was the nearest to a display of anger that Mark was ever likely to come with a customer.

Maddox, though worried, was determined to argue his case. 'That could be the difference between forty-nine and fifty per cent in the end.'

Mark gestured around to the world at large. 'But everyone else must be looking at Maddox's and wondering why there's a sudden interest in your shares. Financial Directors of big engineering firms will be worried in case they're missing something. I bet today there'll be half a dozen discreet enquiries starting about this firm and why it is suddenly so interesting to somebody. Mr Maddox, I do most urgently recommend that you bring in our Merchant Banks subsidiary. If there is no bid, then you still need help to restructure this company to make sure it survives, and if a bid should come, then the Bank will be in a much stronger position to fight it off.'

Maddox thought about it. 'And who would know about this? Would they report directly to me?'

'Well no . . . to your Board. As Chairman of the Board I presume you weren't planning to pay their fees yourself.'

Mark was making sense. Maddox was not so fixed in his ways and attitudes that he could not see that Mark, with his experience of the ways in which large companies operated, was in a far better position to judge the potential threat of a takeover than he was. 'All right. I'll see them. See what they can do. But I am not saying I'll follow their recommendations, you understand.'

On Thursday evening, while Peter was making the most of having the house and Jenny to himself, Sylvia was enjoying her first business trip. The play had been disappointing, but the reception by the theatre Manager and staff had been a delight to her. Obtaining a job had been an excitement in itself, but now she was being made to feel not just that she was working and independent, but that she was important. She pulled her nightdress over her head and hung her clothes up carefully in the wardrobe of the hotel bedroom. It was a good hotel, and the room was softly lit and pleasant. The telephone rang. Sylvia was puzzled as she sat on the bed and answered it. It was Tim Hart.

'Tim. Where are you?' she asked.

'Same as you, sitting in a lonely hotel room.'

Sylvia relaxed back on to the bed and pummelled the pillow behind her head as she spoke. 'How was your play?'

'Terrible! I only stayed for the first act – and that was the longest night I've spent in the theatre for a long time. How was yours?'

Sylvia found herself adopting the same accented style of speaking that Tim was inclined to use. 'Terrible . . . and the second act was worse. It was the longest *two* nights I've ever spent in a theatre.'

Tim chuckled. 'I'm sorry about that,' he said. 'So here we both are, bored . . . if only we were together we could have a glass of champagne, drown our sorrows, and moan about the state of the British theatre.'

'Yes,' Sylvia agreed. 'That would be very nice . . . '

There was a momentary whistling noise on the telephone and the sound of Tim tapping it.

'We must do it some time,' he said.

'Some time,' Sylvia said.

After a pause Tim said, 'Well . . . Good-night . . . '

'Good-night,' Sylvia said warmly, 'I'll see you in the morning.'

'I can't wait . . .'

She lay back smiling to herself for a moment, and then picked up the telephone again. She waited for the switchboard to answer and then gave Mark's number. His voice was drowsy when he answered, and when she looked at her watch she realised it was half past twelve.

'That's all right,' Mark said, sounding a little more awake. 'Did you have a good evening?'

'Actually,' she said, 'the play was terrible. But I did feel very important. The manager made me feel like a queen. How was your day?'

She was interrupted by a knock on the door. A rich Geordie voice boomed through the wood. 'Room service, madam. I've been asked to bring some champagne.'

Mark was saying, 'Hello . . . hello. Hello, Sylvia . . . are you still there . . .'

Sylvia called out to the waiter to hang on for a minute. Then she returned to the telephone. 'It's all right, Mark. I'm sorry about that. It was room service.'

'What on earth did you order?' he demanded.

'Oh . . . some cocoa . . . Look darling, I'm sorry I woke you. Go back to bed. I'll ring you tomorrow. Good-night.'

He wished her good-night and she put the phone down. Sylvia went to the wardrobe and took out her dressing-gown. She was still slipping it on as she opened the door.

Tim Hart stood in the corridor holding a bottle of champagne and two champagne glasses. 'Evening, madam,' he said in the same Geordie voice.

'Tim! What are you . . . you said you were in . . .'

' . . . a lonely hotel room . . .'

'They stood looking at each other. 'You know,' said Tim, 'it's people like you that get guests a bad name from waiters. Don't you want this?'

She stood back from the door and he moved into the room, giving her no opportunity to speak.

'You said it would be very nice, and we could do it sometime, and I said I couldn't wait until tomorrow, to see you, and you didn't disagree and before you make up your mind to be angry with me, just let me say I'm expecting no payment of any kind, for the champagne, or a mad drive over the Pennines, just that you drink a glass with me and wish me a civil good-night and I'll be gone ...'

He covered his urgent need to draw breath by drawing the cork from the bottle. He held the cork to prevent it ricocheting round the room and caught the first foam from the champagne in one of the glasses.

'No strings. Promise,' he said, looking at her. Sylvia closed the door.

'Have you really been to Manchester?' she asked.

Tim pretended to be hurt. 'Do you doubt me, madam?' He produced half a theatre ticket from his pocket, and held it out to her. 'Note the date . . . Ah, *but*, you say, I could have got this from the theatre before tonight. So . . . exhibit two.' He produced from the breast pocket of his suit a small but formal piece of paper, and went on, 'I have to produce my driving licence at West Central in the next five days. I was caught speeding on the M62. Note the time . . . 9.45 p.m. . . . my case rests, m'lady.'

Sylvia burst out laughing. He was too outrageous to deserve the chill reception that she should perhaps have given him. Then he laughed too, and quickly poured champagne in the glasses.

'Tim, you're an idiot,' she said.

He handed her a glass. 'I'm not prepared to defend myself against that charge. Cheers!'

'Cheers!' she said. 'But why did you do it?'

Tim waved his champagne glass expressively, 'I told you . . . the first act was terrible . . . and the prospect of a 120 mile drive for a glass of champagne with you seemed infinitely more exciting.'

'I don't know what to say,' Sylvia remarked, and meant it.

'Well, for starters you could say . . . "Tim you must be terribly tired after that drive, why don't you sit down. Just for a minute mind you. I'm not offering anything but a chair!"'

Sylvia muttered an apology and gestured towards an armchair. She sat on the bed.

'Now, what was our plan?' Tim asked.

'*Your* plan.'

'No *our* plan. We were going to moan about the state of the British theatre, I believe. How was your play?'

Sylvia dismissed the play with a grimace. 'A mess. The

jokes were weak, the structure predictable, and the sentiment phoney.'

'We could buy that and have another West End hit on our hands,' said Tim.

'You said on that first day that only good plays stood a chance now,' she said.

'That's good.' Tim's eyes were flickering between Sylvia's eyes and her knees.

'What's good?' she asked.

'You remembering what I said on the first day.'

'Tim . . . I feel I must say something . . . '

Tim would not let her continue. 'But is it about the British theatre?' he demanded.

'No.'

'Then we mustn't talk about it.' He drained the remainder of the champagne from his glass. 'And in any case I've finished my glass of champagne, so I must go.'

Sylvia was amazed. 'You're going?' she asked.

'Well,' said Tim, 'if you absolutely insist that I stay, I wouldn't be such a boor as to refuse . . . '

Sylvia stood up. 'Good-night then, Tim . . . ' she said.

He left the chair and walked towards the door. She followed him. 'Did you really drive all that way just to drink one glass of champagne?' she asked.

Tim was not alone in saying serious things as a joke and jokey things as serious statements. But on this occasion he plainly meant what he said.

'Sylvia I'm not 16. I'm not into *just* a quick roll in the hay. I like you very much, and I want you to *know* you can trust what I say.'

Tim leaned forward and kissed her lightly and tenderly on the lips. Then he let himself out of the door and closed it quietly.

* * *

While Tim was finishing his breakfast, Sylvia went through to reception. The girl turned from her accounts and Sylvia said, 'I'm just checking that you are sending my bill to Tim Hart Productions. I'm Mrs Telford.'

The girl glanced at her list. 'Yes, that's right,' she said.

'Oh, and . . . Mr Hart . . . what are the arrangements for his bill?' Sylvia asked.

Again the girl checked and looked up. 'The same. The

rooms were booked at the same time.'

Sylvia smiled and went up to her room to finish her packing.

Mark was talking into his dictaphone when he was interrupted by Keith Everly. Keith came into the room with his copy of the *Financial Times*. Mark had come in early to get his notes cleared out of the way and had not yet looked at the paper.

'Have you seen it?' asked Keith. 'Maddox are up another six points!'

'Six!'

'That's right!'

Keith handed the pink newspaper to Mark, who looked at it in horror. 'That's a hell of a rise! I think I'd better get on to Miller. He's already given Maddox one good talking-to.' Miller was from the Bank's Corporate Finance Division.

'Maddox must have ordered a lot of shares,' Keith observed.

'If he's the only buyer.'

Mark put the handset of the dictaphone down onto the desk and reached for the telephone. Miller said that he'd slipped a word into the ear of the Bank's brokers to see if they could find out discreetly on the floor of the Stock Exchange who else might be buying shares. It now looked as though the price rise was more than could simply be explained by Maddox's panic buying of his own stock. Miller thought the situation was sufficiently worrying to warrant a trip down to Dover for another meeting with Maddox that afternoon, if Mark could arrange it.

Mark rang off and asked Carol to get Maddox on the line straight away. She returned a few minutes later to say that Maddox wasn't at the factory. He had not been in that morning.

'That's very strange,' said Mark. 'He prides himself on not missing a day.'

Carol returned immediately to say that Mr Maddox had arrived at the Bank and wanted to see Mark at once.

'What have I got today?' he asked her.

'Eleven-thirty, Mr Fiske. You've no luncheon appointment. Three o'clock a Mr & Mrs Elton about a bridging loan.'

Mark thought for a moment. 'Keith, you take Mr Fiske will you? He's thinking of forming himself into a company . . . and the Eltons, I don't know anything about them. And Carol, you'd better keep me clear, if possible. Just stay for a moment Carol, will you. I want to check with Maddox if he's free this afternoon.'

Mark went out into the hall of the bank and greeted the heavy-faced factory owner. He led Maddox back into his office.

'I think I know why you've come, Mr Maddox. Mr Miller has been on the phone this morning and he would like to see you this afternoon. Could you manage that?'

'Yes, I can.'

Mark dispatched Carol to make the arrangements, and when she closed the door after her, asked whether Maddox had seen the paper that morning.

'Yes. I haven't ordered any more shares since last week, so it looks as though there are some bloody pirates in the market!'

'Well,' said Mark reassuringly, 'they do have a considerable job. If you keep control of your block they won't find it easy. But Mr Miller will know far more than I do about this sort of thing.'

Maddox remained standing. 'Will you lend me £100,000?' he asked.

Mark looked at him in astonishment. 'Why?'

'To buy shares.'

'Aren't we being a little precipitate?' said Mark. 'Perhaps we should wait to see Mr Miller.'

'Will you lend me the money?' Maddox demanded.

'What sort of security were you thinking of offering?'

Maddox sat down now. 'I have an endowment policy maturing in 5 years for £30,000. There are my shares in the company and my house. That's worth £60,000.'

'But just a minute,' said Mark. 'How could you afford the interest repayments, let alone the capital requirements? At present, with the rates at their very lowest, we should be looking for three over base rate, say 10%. That would mean £10,000 a year interest – and we would also be looking for say, £10,000 repayment – that would be £20,000 a year.'

Maddox had not considered it in that light. 'Well I could run down the reserves a bit and pay the shareholders a bonus,' he began.

Mark cut across him firmly. 'Do you realise how much? That £20,000 – and that's only the first year – is not tax deductable. So you would have to give yourself over £100,000 to leave £20,000 clear, and as you own only 20% of the firm that means you would have to declare a dividend totalling well over half a million.'

'Income Tax!' Maddox shouted. 'The buggers have got you every way! Couldn't we just pay the Directors?'

Mark smiled. 'If you voted yourself that sort of money there would be a legal action against you from the other shareholders, at least! The Company can't buy its own shares, as you know.' Mark paused a moment before continuing. He did not like the trend of Maddox's thoughts. 'Mr Maddox, you are now, by any standards, a wealthy man. I do urge you not to damage yourself by acting hastily. Look, you want to buy shares on a steeply rising market. If you succeed in your aim, the shares would almost certainly fall – they must do – below the price they started at a few weeks ago. Overnight you would lose 20% or 25% of your capital investment. I know you are doing this to keep your company but even that is not certain. You must bear in mind that we started this whole exercise because I was worried about the long term viability of your company.'

'That's your opinion,' said Maddox in a tone which made it clear that he did not agree.

'Yes, it is,' Mark went on, 'and I have to make a judgement on it. If we *should* have to recall the loan or if interest rates doubled – as they did a year or so ago – we should find ourselves in a situation where you could not possibly manage the interest and capital repayments – and the Bank would have to evict the town's biggest business man – and sell his house. We'd rather not get ourselves into that position.'

Maddox considered this. 'And so you'll only lend on the insurance policy?' he asked.

'Providing you can satisfy us you could pay the interest,

we might be able to lend you, say, £30,000 with interest repayments of say £3,000 a year, and no capital repayments for the first 3 years.'

Maddox was not pleased with this offer, and said they would talk about it after he had spoken to Mr Miller that afternoon.

Sylvia and Tim were back in the office before she told of her detective work at the hotel.

'Oh dear,' he said. 'It's always the same. If the lady is bright enough to be really attractive, she's bright enough to see through one's little ruses. But, in my defence, I must say, I didn't say any different.'

'No, I know. I thought over what you did say and you didn't lie . . . technically at least.'

Tim was being serious again. 'More than that. Look I *had* to go to Manchester but I *knew* it would be bloody awful . . . if, by a chance in a million, it hadn't been I would have stayed.'

'There's no need to explain.'

'You're not cross about last night?' he asked.

'Nothing happened, did it?'

'You don't have to rub it in . . . behaving like a gentleman can be a real strain on the nervous system you know.'

Sylvia smiled. 'But you did, and I'm grateful,' she said.

He kissed her lightly on the cheek and very quickly went out into his own office, shutting the door after him. Sylvia was shaken by this. It was more confusing to have him behave like a gentleman than it would have been if he had behaved like a rapist brute.

She turned to the telephone on her desk, dialed through to Dover, and interrupted Mark, who was just leaving his office with Mr Miller, to ask him if he would come home for dinner that evening.

'What's wrong?' Mark asked.

'Nothing's wrong,' she said, 'nothing at all. I'd just like to see you, that's all. Is that so surprising?'

Mark said he would be very pleased to come home, and hurried off to his meeting.

As she was putting the phone down, Tim came back

into the office. 'Sorry, I didn't realise you were on the phone,' he said.

'It's all right . . . I've finished . . . I was just ringing Mark to ask him to come home to dinner tonight.'

'Oh. Nice,' Tim said carefully. 'And he's coming?'

'Yes.'

'Good. I hope you have a lovely evening.'

'Yes, I shall,' said Sylvia.

She smiled at him, and after a moment he returned her smile and went back to his own office.

Mark Telford, Christopher Maddox and his father sat in the bleak office at Maddox Engineering and began their meeting with Mr Miller, a tall, good-looking man in his mid-thirties who had obviously done all his homework on Maddox.

'Let's start at the beginning,' the expert in company finance began. 'What we have here is virtually a one-product company . . . '

It was not too early in his speech for Maddox to interrupt. 'That's a bit strong, isn't it?' he said.

Miller continued. 'According to your last year's figures, nearly 80% of your turnover came from the sale of the gas valve. Now, apart from the fact that a single invention could render your product obsolete, you have not made any significant productivity progress that I can see from the figures for years. It follows that you are becoming less and less competitive as other companies invest in research and development. The first thing to be said, therefore, is that if you are to remain an independent company, you ought to invest pretty heavily in research to increase productivity on your basic product. Secondly, you ought to be looking for new products to diversify your production to allow for the time when the valve phases out . . . '

Maddox interrupted again. 'Well, Telford's told me all that before, and I've started looking into it . . . we can manage that . . . '

Miller was not a man to be diverted that simply. 'But that will take time. The indications are that we don't have years or even months to do that. I must tell you I anticipate an approach to you with an offer to sell in the very near future. If the sale is not agreed, then there will probably be an unfriendly bid.'

Maddox smacked his fist down on his desk, shaking his coffee cup. 'We'll bloody well fight them, won't we Christopher? '

Christopher was not so definite as his father. 'I suppose so,' he said. 'How much do you think we could sell for, Mr Miller?'

'What the hell difference does it make?' Maddox roared, before Miller could reply.

'Don't be silly, dad,' said Christopher. 'We ought to know all the facts.'

They both turned back to Miller, who went on, 'Obviously I haven't done nearly enough work on this, but from my first sight of turnover and profit and loss – and particularly your assets, which Mr Telford tells me are undervalued, I think we could sell each share for something like a little over £2.'

Christopher Maddox betrayed no emotion. '£2 . . . that values the company at a million. So my share would be worth £100,000!'

His father was growing impatient with this talk. 'What difference does it make?' he yelled. 'We're not selling! Look Mr Miller, I keep trying to tell you. I own a little over 20%. Chris here has 10%. My younger son's 10% is in trust for him when he's 25 and my uncle has the income from 10% in trust to come to the boys when he dies. That makes over 50% as I've said. They can't win.

Miller looked up from his analysis to face the industrialist. 'You've not thought of one thing. 20% of that 50% is in trust. The trustees may decide that the trust beneficiaries' money would be better safeguarded if this company became part of a larger, more progressive company.'

Maddox laughed. 'But the trustees are our bank. Knight's Bank. We've been with them for years. They wouldn't sell, would they Telford?'

Mark was now treading a conversational minefield. 'I don't know for certain, but you do not in any way control those shares. The trustees have a duty in law to act solely in the interest of their beneficiaries. And if they felt that the money would be safer and would earn more dividend in another company, they must sell, or they could be sued for negligence by the beneficiaries.'

'My uncle is a ga-ga,' Maddox said. 'He won't sue. And do you think my sons would sue, against me?'

Mark continued in the same careful tone of voice. 'It doesn't make any difference Mr Maddox. The Bank wouldn't act on the basis that your uncle was senile and therefore wouldn't avail himself of a proper legal remedy. They would act as they saw fit in his interests, and those of your son.'

Maddox sat back in his chair and looked around the room. 'What loyalty, eh?' he said. 'We've banked with Knight's for years, from the beginning, and now when there's a real need, they turn into rats deserting the ship. Well I'll tell you something. If we lose this battle, you've lost our account.'

'We shall in any case,' said Mark. 'We know that the company that's likely to make the bid is Western Foundries. They bank with the Midland. They'll transfer it there.'

'And knowing that, you'll still help to destroy this company,' Maddox said.

'I think the bank would take the view that they were helping to save it, and in any case, they would have an absolute duty to protect the beneficiaries, whatever happened to the account.'

Maddox stood up and walked round the room. 'All right.' he said, 'Now you listen. I don't care what anyone else does, we're going to fight. If you won't lend me the money to buy shares, then I'll find someone who will. I'll sell every bloody thing I have to buy shares in this company, and live in this sodding office if necessary. Now, just tell me one thing more: if I manage to get mine and Chris's holding up to 40%, would they succeed in a bid?'

Mark gestured to Miller for an answer.

'38%?'

'Touch and go.'

Maddox stood in front of them. 'All right!' he shouted. 'So I know what to do.'

'Mr Maddox, it's madness,' said Miller. 'You could lose everything.'

The tiny veins on Maddox's cheeks were now plainly visible. Miller was wondering whether he was about to witness a heart attack, as well as a takeover bid.

'Well, my father was mad!' shouted Maddox again, 'Thinking he could build a business that would grow to be worth a million, starting with a hundred pounds capital. But he did it, and I'm not going to let it go!'

He strode to the door, threw it open and gestured for them to go through it. As Mark and Miles went out, Christopher Maddox was still sitting in his chair staring at the ceiling.

As they walked across the car park, Miller said 'I wouldn't trust young Christopher further than I could throw him.'

'No,' said Mark. 'It's such a common pattern though, isn't it? He's not a bad man, Maddox; autocratic, obstinate, but he's worked and sweated.'

Miller opened the door of the car and leaned through it to unlock the passenger door for Mark. 'You don't run a company with sweat,' he said. 'The skills are very different. You need flexibility, vision, and the ability to prune hard at dead wood. Some of the very qualities that make Maddox an attractive man – his paternalism – makes him a bad managing director.'

Mark climbed into the car. 'I think he's got a point though . . . efficiency isn't everything. He looks after his men for example. I think they really respect him.'

Miller started the engine. 'Of course,' he said, 'but when his company goes bust his workers will be the first to shout that he's failed them. They won't proclaim their love for him from the dole queue.'

When he had finished his share of the duck and Valpolicella, Peter went out to the inevitable rock group practice. Sylvia looked across the table at Mark. 'It's good to have you home again,' she said.

'Thank you,' Mark replied. 'It was a good meal. I particularly liked the fatted calf.'

They were back at their fencing again. 'Why?' riposted

Sylvia, 'Are you the prodigal? Been consorting etc., in Dover?'

Mark smiled wryly. 'Yes, with shopkeepers who want more shelves, couples who want a house, and a sub-lieutenant of industry who wants to keep his company. And before you ask, yes I do want to stay.'

'Until all the shopkeepers have shelves, all the couples have houses and the sub-lieutenant becomes the captain of industry?'

'Actually,' said Mark, 'he's more likely to be cashiered and reduced to the ranks. But what about your job? Still enjoying it?'

He had no need to ask. Sylvia was radiant. 'Oh yes, I am! More than anything for years really. And it's not just the money, it's feeling part of the world again. When I see a theatre somewhere I look at what they are doing, looking for new plays, new names. It's silly really, I suppose. It's the feeling of power. I mean this morning, I saw a poster outside the Oxford Playhouse. It was advertising . . . '

'Oxford?' Mark asked, cutting across her.

'On my way back from Newcastle.'

Mark stuttered slightly as he said, 'I thought you went up by train.'

Sylvia realised Mark's tack. 'I did . . . Tim drove me back. He'd gone up North too . . . he picked me up and drove me back. Simple. Anyway, at the Playhouse . . . ' She got no further before Mark interrupted again.

'When did he pick you up?'

'Last night.'

'I see.'

'I don't think you do, Mark.'

Mark stirred his coffee. 'And the "room service" last night?'

Sylvia had decided that the only course open to her now was complete honesty. If Mark detected the faintest smell of a half-truth it would be critical. 'Yes, that was Tim . . . ' she said. 'I was completely taken by surprise, I promise you.'

There was an unusually hard edge to Mark's usually soft voice as he commented, 'I didn't know you meant the word "service" so agriculturally.'

Sylvia put her coffee cup down carefully and said, 'Mark, you had better listen to me before you say something that you will regret later.'

Mark sipped his coffee. 'I'm listening,' he said.

'Tim went to a theatre in Manchester last night. He left after the first act and came over to see me.'

Mark smiled. 'To bring you cocoa!'

'No. Champagne if you must know.'

Mark nodded as though with approval. 'He has style.'

They looked at each other. Mark's expression was not a pleasant one.

'Yes, he has,' Sylvia agreed. 'He made it clear that he would like to sleep with me, with "great style", and I made it clear, equally stylishly I hope, that it wasn't on. We had one glass of champagne and he returned to his room after a formal kiss. That was all. This morning we drove down and stopped for a very pleasant lunch in Oxford.'

Mark continued in the same bitter vein. 'So why all the guilt . . .the loving phone call, the summons home, the Duck a L'Orange.'

Sylvia thought that she had already been as honest as she would have to be, but now she realised that she would have to transcend the history and talk about the motivation. 'Because I have a fear,' she said, 'that if Tim had been only one jot less "stylish", one iota more pressing, I would have finished up in bed with him.'

'You wanted to?' Mark half-asked and half-stated.

'Yes . . . with a part of me . . . I wanted to very much.'

Mark's voice was now soft, but there was no mistaking its barbs. 'And if you had, would one act of adultery have finished us?'

Sylvia was trying to keep this within the boundaries of an intimate but abstract discussion. 'No . . . not necessarily,' she said. 'We've never really discussed this . . . I don't know if you've ever been unfaithful to me. I don't want to know. Really, I mean it. I don't want to know. As it happens, I have never been unfaithful to you, but that's almost irrelevant. There have been occasions when I was very tempted and if I had . . . yielded . . . it wouldn't have threatened us at all.'

There was a pause. Mark put his coffee cup down gently and said, 'But last night was different.'

Sylvia had the feeling that she was drawing back from this conversation. Although one level of her personality was taking part in it and discussing it with Mark, at another level she was a spectator watching the proceedings, watching the truth being prised out of her completely against her will.

She said, 'Yes, it was different . . . because I like Tim. I like him very much.'

'Are you telling me you love Tim?' Mark asked. All trace of his stutter had now gone from his voice.

'No I'm not. I'm telling you I think I could, and if we made love I would. I'm telling you I feel we, as a couple, are threatened, and I want *us* to fight back.'

'How?' Mark said angrily. 'By giving up Dover? By coming back to London? It's blackmail, Sylvia!'

She was also now becoming angry. 'No, it's not. That's a terrible thing to say! Can't you see, I'm struggling to save us. We have to look for each other again.'

Mark's anger intensified. 'That's not hard is it? You know where I am. Where I've always been. I can't match your sexy young theatre manager with his glamorous job . . .'

Sylvia interrupted him. 'You're insulting me Mark,' she said more gently, but still with a stiffening of anger, 'I know what you are and I love you. As a matter of fact I've always found you the wittiest, most attractive man I've ever met. I love your compassion, softness if you like . . . but these are ideals in my head now. I know they're true because I tell myself they're true. But I didn't need to do that once. Now I do.'

Mark left the table and began to pace up and down. She watched him.

'So what do you want us to do?' he asked.

'I don't know. I suppose I started by bringing it all out into the open. My "Oxford" slip was almost certainly Freudian.'

'Yes,' he said, his back turned on her. 'Thank you for that . . .'

Sylvia pushed her chair back and went over to him. He was standing with one hand on the tall mantelpiece. He looked as though he were instinctively shielding himself from a blow.

'We have to look for each other again!' she said, putting her hand on his back.

He moved away from her. He looked at the ceiling. 'Sylvia, you are one of the most honest people I've ever met. I love you too. I want you to think and answer this honestly. Is all this "looking for each other" – whatever that means – a way of coping with your guilt when we don't find each other?'

She now took his place by the mantelpiece. She wished she could get near him. She wished he would not retreat, not at this moment when she had found the resolve to say the things which had been in her mind all day. Why should he hide himself away and refuse the touch that she was proffering?

She said, 'I suppose it could be, it hadn't occurred to me . . . but if you don't have faith in us, Mark, we may as well finish tonight.'

They stood still for a long time, how long neither of them could tell. In the relativity of that moment, time was as meaningless as gesture. They were both utterly alone, needing the comfort of each other, but held apart by all that had gone before.

'I'll get on with the washing up,' Sylvia said as a last attempt to crack through the shell. Still Mark said nothing, so she took the plates from the table and went away with them.

When Mark arrived back late at the bank in Dover the next morning with a headache, there was a message from Maddox. The Financial Director of Western Foundries would be calling on him at 10.30. Maddox wanted Mr Telford to attend.

Mark put his coat back on and twenty minutes later hurried from a taxi to the depressing office building of Maddox Engineering.

Mr Calthorpe of Western Foundries was a rugged-faced man in his fifties. Mark hurried into the meeting and was grudgingly introduced.

'This is Calthorpe from Western Foundries,' said Maddox. 'He's come to offer me 205p per share, and he's in the middle of telling me that when he takes us over, he'll want to keep me, but he'll want his financial man here, his methods and organisation man, his work and efficiency expert, and research director. But he'll still want me. Oh yes, he'll still want me because they'll need somebody to lick the bloody stamps!'

'Oh, Mr Maddox, that's going a bit far,' said Calthorpe.

'I want 220!' shouted Maddox.

'That's too much, I'm afraid,' said Calthorpe. 'We have looked . . . '

'How much?' demanded Maddox.

Calthorpe was hesitant. He might have been giving away free samples of diamonds. 'We might go to 210,' he said.

'Make it 212 and it's yours,' said Maddox. Proud, bitter, and defiant in defeat.

'I'll put it to the board, but I think I can say . . . '

'Just send the offer!' Maddox shouted.

Calthorpe tried to placate Maddox. 'I'm sure we can look forward . . . '

Maddox moved dangerously close to the other man and shouted in a voice that could be heard echoing round the court-yard, 'All right, you've got what you wanted, now just bugger off!'

'I do understand . . . ' Calthorpe began again.

'Bugger off!'

Calthorpe left his chair, picked up his briefcase and went to the door. 'Good morning Mr Telford,' he said, and went out.

Maddox sat down in his chair and rubbed his head with his hands. Mark had never seen such distraction in his face. 'I'm sorry Mr Maddox . . . but I'm sure you've done the right thing.'

Maddox's frustration became focused on Mark. 'The only thing left . . . I can see the bank had to stab me in the back. It's heart *is* in a strong room after all. But last night, Christopher told me he was going to sell.'

Maddox was certainly not a man to cry, but despite the clear and ironic way he said this, Mark could tell that he had been deeply hurt. Everything that he valued in his life he had lost, or it had rejected him.

'I'm sorry,' Mark said quietly.

'When you put your faith in someone, Telford, and then

you find that they're up to the highest bidder it's not worth a candle . . . don't you think?'

Mark looked from poor Maddox to the photograph of his father that hung on the wall behind his desk. They had nothing more to say to each other. Mark turned and followed Calthorpe from the room, feeling sad, unworthy, and guilty.

Chapter Seven

October began as though all the zephyrs of the atmosphere were conspiring to blow the waters of the Channel down the chimneys of Dover and Folkestone; and then settled into an exhausted calm. Those of Mark's customers who were able to replace shattered tiles or could nail a few planks into a fence, showed healthy cash flows. The computer terminal in the branch fell to an untraceable paralysis that wrought its own windless havoc on the paper-work. Money was lent and money recouped. The base lending rate went up half a per cent, and the Clearing Banks followed it after a brief pause designed to assert their independence from the Bank of England.

Manton's, the giant French multi-national that was in part responsible for Mark's retreat to the south coast, put its first Norman invader into Britain in the form of a Monsieur Dieber, who was both a competent businessman, and a good lunch companion. He swiftly lived up to the stereotype of a French passion by falling in love with the widowed Helen Santon in whose hotel he was staying.

Carol passed her A.I.B. exams and Keith was so impressed that, on the spur of the moment, or spurred by the champagne, he asked her to marry him. She agreed.

The relationship between Mark and Sylvia was like that of intimate pen pals who were embarrassed and disappointed when they met.

Sylvia and Tim Hart distanced themselves not by miles

and telephones, but by a parody of courtly love. Style was all. Style was the joy, the temptation, and ultimately the safety-valve. When Tim pressed just *too* hard, Sylvia clapped and patted his head and declined any role in his life but that of *belle dame sans merci*. She enjoyed his attentions as one who enjoys music; but one must not let the melody shatter the windows of one's life into fragments. She needed all the certainty she could command to deal with Peter. He was finding less and less time for school work and his mock 'A' levels were only months away.

Mark had become accustomed to the duality of his life. When he visited his wife and son he was, or tried to be, a relaxed man who had acted in the way he thought best. In Dover he had laid the invisible tracks of a settled routine. The cottage was lonely, but he felt no inclination to seek any new relationship. He read; Proust and Solzhenitzin, Jane Austen and John Updike. Very occasionally he went with two colleagues to a concert or play in Canterbury.

He missed his piano. Sometimes when he was thinking in his office, he found his fingers forming chords on the edge of his desk. But even if there had been room in the small cottage for the piano, he could not have removed it from his London house. It would have seemed to Sylvia far too symbolic an action. He examined a few second-hand uprights on sale in the local music shop, but their touch seemed heavy after the grand, so he tried to put that out of his mind. If he could not play, he could at least listen to music. He bought a stereo system from an electronics warehouse run by one of his customers, and installed that in the cottage.

Every free lunch time, when the wind was not too ferocious, he walked down to the harbour and watched the pleasure boats and fishing boats swinging on their warps. If he could not have his piano, surely Sylvia would see the logic of him bringing his sloop to this harbour, where he could paint it and refurbish it? She and Peter could come down on fine weekends, and they could sail across the Channel, along the French coast. Of course, he would need Sylvia to crew for him on the trip round the bulge of Kent.

So it was that in mid-October, Sylvia found herself

struggling with a heavy shopping bag over the dyke of a creek on the Blackwater and looking down at Mark who was adjusting the rigging on their sloop. He was busy with the rope, smiling and whistling to himself. He looked happier than she had seen him for a long time. The sun was well down in the west and the evening light was thickening like varnish on an old landscape. She heaved the bags down the slope, taking care not to slip on the loose soil, and walked to the bank. Mark was unaware of her arrival. She watched him knotting and checking, still whistling.

'Hello sailor!' she called.

Mark looked up startled. 'Sylvia, I didn't see you coming.'

'Of course not,' she called. 'When a man is busy with his mistress he is not aware of his wife . . . '

Mark gestured around the boat. 'She looks good, doesn't she?'

Indeed she did. The gear on the forward deck was neatly coiled and arranged by Mark and the paintwork was trim.

'As soon as I get aboard,' called Mark, 'I always wonder why on earth I've stayed away so long . . . why on earth I bother with golf or even banking. Why we don't just sail away for ever.'

Sylvia set the shopping bag down. 'Before you *do* cast off, do you think I should come aboard? It would be an awful anti-climax if you had to come back for me.'

Mark apologised for his babbling and stepped off the boat to help her on. As their combined weight tilted the deck, the boat bobbed in the water, a moving, living sensation that was pure joy to Mark.

He hefted the bag in his hand. 'Goodness me, what on earth have you got in there?' he asked.

'Most of the tins in the cupboard. I've been on these weekends before, remember. They have been known to last till Tuesday.'

Mark shook his head. 'This one won't. I must be in Dover by Monday.'

They went below to the cramped but cosy cabin. In the warm glow of the oil lamp, Sylvia stood looking at the table Mark had laid, complete with wine, rolls, and a delicious looking salad. The delicious aroma of cooking wafted through from the tiny galley. They equipped themselves with sherry and drank a little toast to a happy trip. Sylvia told Mark that Peter had changed his mind at the last minute and decided that he would come after all, but she had asked him not to. She wanted them to have a weekend alone. Peter had been quite paternal about it. He had almost patted her on the head and sent her off to have a good weekend.

'It's terrifying how quickly they grow up,' Mark observed.

'Yes,' Sylvia replied, squeezing herself into one of the small seats. 'If they do ever. Sometimes I think I've never grown up. Do you ever get that feeling?'

Mark threw his head back to consider. 'In a way I suppose I do. I can't remember feeling any different than I do now, but I must have. When I look at Peter and think "when I was his age, I'd already spent a year working in the bank", it doesn't seem possible that I was so callow. It seemed to me then as if I was completely the master of my fate.'

Sylvia sipped her sherry. 'Do you still feel that?' she asked.

Mark hesitated. The smile left his face for the first time. 'No . . . no, I don't.'

'But you've changed your life quite deliberately, in a way you couldn't have when you were seventeen.'

Again Mark considered. 'I have the illusion that I have, certainly.'

'More than an illusion surely?' Sylvia asked.

Mark made an indefinite gesture. 'Oh, one acts,' he said, 'and changes occur, but they would in any case. And the changes that flow from the action are not the ones you plan. So the control over the mastery of one's fate is an illusion. It could only be a reality if you could foresee – and plan for – all the changes that result from the deliberate act.'

Mark went to fetch the food. Sylvia poured out the wine and they began to eat. There was still a tension between them that was not being expressed. It was like a taut wire carrying unwanted vibrations.

'So, Skipper, what's your plan for getting us to Dover?' Sylvia asked, diverting the chat to less difficult waters.

Mark smiled again. 'Well, if the forecast is right, and we

get the force 3 or 4 sou'wester, I reckon it will take us about 20–25 hours. I want to arrive at Dover in the light, so I thought we'd have a long lie-in tomorrow – if we can – and cast off around 11.00. I'd like to do it in one go if possible. There aren't any really decent harbours and I'm never happy moored off a beach.'

'Will it be safe?' Sylvia asked. 'It's a terribly busy waterway.'

'Busiest in the world. We'll just have to keep our eyes peeled, that's all. Well, how's your week gone?'

Sylvia explained at some lengths over the meal the difficulties they were experiencing in bringing the play *No Earthly Reason* into London. Mark was not surprised that it was causing a problem; anyone who could write a play with such an appalling title hardly deserved fame and fortune. Whenever she spoke of work and plays, Sylvia was bubbly and effusive, and it continued to irritate Mark.

'What's Tim like?' he asked.

'Pleasant-looking. Forties. Forty-three, actually.'

'That's very accurate.'

'I looked him up in *Who's Who*.'

Mark dropped his eyes to the meal. He sliced a potato with more energy than it deserved. 'I see,' he said.

Sylvia looked at him across the table. 'You're very tense, Mark, aren't you?'

Mark lifted his eyes. 'How important is he? To you, I mean.'

Sylvia began to extol his virtues as a theatrical manager and an employer but she realised that that was not what Mark wanted to hear. 'I still haven't slept with him, if that's what you mean,' she said. 'Mark you're being . . . foolish. We both know what this weekend is about. Let's see if we can get ourselves back . . . on an even keel, so to speak. We won't do that if there's another man in the boat with us . . . to unbalance us. Mark, everything's suddenly topsy-turvy. No one's behaving true to type . . . you, me . . . '

Before he could stop himself Mark snapped, 'Tim Hart probably is!' and was instantly sorry for the remark. He apologised.

'If we're going to continue this for the whole weekend,' Sylvia said, 'it would be better for both our sakes if we called the trip off now. Mark, you have to trust me. Believe me, please. I want us to succeed.'

Mark put his knife and fork down, leaving a third of the food uneaten. 'Yes,' he said. 'It's just that, it's hard to find oneself in a sort of adolescent competition in middle age . . . '

'What's so adolescent about it?' she demanded. 'There's no law that I know of – natural cr man-made – that guarantees that once you've bedded or impregnated a woman, all competition ceases and you can lie back and relax for the rest of your life.'

Mark picked up his knife and fork again. 'I took you for granted, you mean?' he asked.

Sylvia nodded. 'Yes – well, didn't you?'

He returned the knife and fork to his plate. 'Perhaps . . . but isn't that right? Inevitable even? I don't mean . . . exhibit a cruel disregard, but that when life goes on, broadens out, work becomes more challenging, difficult, enjoyable even, perhaps . . . and that's right. Surely you don't have to spend all your time watching your wife to make sure no one steals her away.'

Despite her effort to speak softly and avoid them falling into that awful pit of recrimination, there was a snap in her voice as she said, 'Your language is so revealing Mark. You can only steal possessions.'

'Or affections,' he said.

'No, affections can't be stolen, only earned.'

Mark squeezed out from behind the small table and took his plate into the galley.

'Aren't you going to finish it?' she asked.

There was no reply but the sound of him scraping the remains off his plate into the waste bucket. He went up from the saloon and into the cockpit and stood watching the light die over the water. The breeze was rising into the sou'westerly for which he had been hoping. A flight of river birds circled over the creek and settled into a reed bed. Sylvia came up the steps and through the hatch. She was carrying two glasses of wine.

'At least you'll finish this?' she asked.

Mark took the glass from her. 'Yes,' he said. 'Thank you. I'm sorry, Sylvia, I really am. I don't know what's come over me!'

Sylvia stood beside him and looked out over the water. 'Well . . . not being too profound about it I'd say it was a simple case of jealousy.'

'Pathetic isn't it,' he said wryly.

'I don't think so. I would be exactly the same.'

He smiled at her more openly. 'That's generous,' he said.

She smiled back at him and perched on the side of the cockpit. 'It is beautiful here. So quiet. Will it be as good in Dover harbour?'

'Not so quiet – much nearer France.'

'I thought you were fed up with travelling,' she nudged.

'Flying isn't travelling. The aeroplane annihilates distance and international trade destroys national differences. I mean what would you rather do, zoom over to Paris and book in at the Paris Hilton, which is indistinguishable from any other Hilton, or sail over the Channel to a little Normandy fishing harbour. Go ashore, tired and hungry, to a little pension, eat the home cooked food of the Patronne and sleep the sleep of the exhausted in a huge feather bed.'

Sylvia laughed. 'Would it sound terribly disloyal if I opted for the Jet and the Hilton? I do understand what you mean, but you've "jetted" to Paris and stayed in the Hilton so often, *and* you are an incurable romantic. I'm surprised you settled for Dover. I wouldn't have been surprised if you'd thrown up your job altogether and set off to . . . sail around the world.'

Mark made as though to cast off the warps. 'What an excellent idea! . . . ' he said. 'Coming?'

'No! I've only just got a job, remember.'

Mark's burst of energy subsided. 'Can I forget?'

'But this job *is* sailing round the world for me, Mark.'

They looked out over the rise and fall of the water as the light dimmed to pewter, bronze and finally blue velvet, and the first stars appeared.

'Would you like to go to the pub for a drink?' Mark asked.

'If you really want to. But I'm very tired and we have a long day tomorrow.'

'A twenty-four hour day in fact.'

'I'll get ready for bed, then.'

Sylvia went below and Mark stayed just a little longer looking out over the river. He was just going to follow Sylvia down to bed when the headlights and roar of a car pierced the gloom and the silence. The car drew to a halt out of sight behind the dyke. He heard the slamming of doors, and the unmistakable silhouette of Peter appeared over the top of the bank, followed closely by Jenny.

'Dad!' he called.

'Peter! What on earth are you doing here?'

'Just visiting!' Peter called. 'Come on Jenny!'

The two young people ran down the dyke to the mooring.

Mark put his head into the companion way and called to Sylvia that her fledgling had found his way to their temporary nest by the water. The two ran panting to the bank and Peter invited Jenny to comment on the beauty of the sloop. She was impressed.

'We can only stay five minutes . . . it took longer than we thought,' she said.

'Jenny passed her driving test today Dad,' Peter said.

'Congratulations!' Mark called. 'You'd better come on board.'

Mark called down to Sylvia to see if she was decent. She was pulling an anorak over her nightdress. Mark descended and Peter and Jenny followed.

It was snug and crowded in the saloon. Mark made them all sit down because he found it a little overwhelming when more than one person stood. They stayed for ten minutes, Peter finishing the bottle of wine and Jenny, who had no desire to be breathalised on her first day as a driver, sipped a bitter lemon.

Peter, aware of the fact that Jenny could borrow her father's car to take them out for a spin, whereas he could not, wondered whether he might take Jenny sailing sometime.

'If you pass your sailing test,' Mark said.

'There's no such thing,' Peter replied.

'On my boat there is – and I'm a pretty stiff examiner.'

Peter nodded. It was a challenge. 'The next time there's a force 6 or 7, I'll come down and take you out in the Channel and show you I can handle her,' he said.

After a little more cheerful banter, Jenny and Peter

climbed back over the dyke and the sound of the car roared away into the silence. Sylvia stood shivering in the cockpit beside Mark as they watched the headlights fade. 'Suddenly I feel very old,' she said.

'So do I.'

'I suppose we had as much energy once,' she said, and turned into the companion way.

* * *

Sylvia was lying in the darkness with her eyes open, thinking quietly. She rolled over to face Mark. He, too, was wide awake, lying with his hands behind his head.

'Can't you sleep?' she asked.

He spoke softly, 'No. I'm enjoying the motion of the boat, and thinking about Peter . . . '

When people talk in the night, pauses that would yawn like inter-stellar space in the daylight seem natural. After a while Sylvia said, 'He seemed very happy.'

'Yes very,' said Mark. 'But don't let me keep you awake . . . '

'It's all right, I was awake anyway.'

'Recently I was talking to Mrs Santon – she's a hotelier – and I suddenly felt very sad. She and her husband in their late twenties had taken on the business and worked and worked and made it really quite successful. Then, when he was only forty-two – bang, all over. And she was left wondering what it was all about, those years of struggle, of building. I mean what is it now? An empty shell! And then looking at Peter and Jenny, full of life, and energy. Driving a hundred and fifty miles on a whim, just because they could . . . their visit here could hardly be said to justify a round trip of a hundred and fifty miles, could it? . . . All that energy would be poured into a life, and at some time in the future, they will suddenly stop and say to themselves, "what have we done – what are we doing?" . . . I wonder what they will be able to answer?'

There was another dark pause. 'What did you answer?' she asked.

Mark couldn't understand the question. 'Me?'

'You're talking about yourself, aren't you?'

She snuggled warmly under the quilt and felt the rocking of the boat lifting, lifting and gently rolling away.

'I suppose so,' Mark went on. 'I answered to myself that my life was like a pattern made by a moving torch in the dark. As long as it kept moving, it was fascinating to watch, making intricate patterns – but when it stopped there was no pattern. Just a pin prick of light glimmering feebly in the dark. I find it hard to accept that my life only has a pattern if I'm on the move.'

Sylvia interrupted him. 'Why?' she asked.

'It's like dancing. When the movement stops there is no dance.'

'And there has to be a dance?'

'Yes.'

'And if one partner wants to waltz, the other partner can take another partner to quick-step.'

Sylvia moved across to him. 'You're torturing yourself Mark. Why?' she asked. 'What do you think I'm doing here. Do you take me for some fickle . . . Oh I don't know! I love you. I know you're going through some sort of crisis . . . you're unhappy, you felt you had to change and you don't know – in your heart – you don't know if you've done the right thing. I understand all that. Why don't you trust me!'

'Oh but I do,' he replied. 'I do trust you. I trust you to be really honest with both of us . . . Yes I am unhappy . . . tell me this . . . are you?'

There was a very long pause. The only sound was the lap of water against the planking.

'No!' Sylvia said eventually.

She moved gently forward and lay her head on his chest. His arm came around her shoulder and squeezed her to him. Unseen by Mark, Sylvia's eyes were full of tears.

The morning dawned bright, sunny and breezy. They made good progress down the coast. Mark stood at the helm on his own for most of the day smiling at the motion and sounds of the boat as the prow split the water and sent it tumbling into a soft wake. The herring gulls rose high above them, swooping now and then low over the deck down to the water that they had searched for fish. From time to time the jib sheet caught on a deck fitting, and then Sylvia took the helm as Mark went on to the forard deck and adjusted it. She watched him standing there holding the forestry and gazing with pride at the bow wave as though it were his own creation.

'You know Mark Telford!' she called, 'you were born 300 years too late. You should have been the master of a little boat setting out to find the spice islands!'

The auspicious day was marred by the evening. The navigation lights refused to work, and as the sun set over Kent it became more and more crucial. Mark had lost his smile and was swearing and cursing. He was a meticulous and careful sailor and had checked the lights before they had left.

At last they could go no farther. They had no alternative but to go inshore and ride out the night, with an emergency paraffin lamp to warn passing ships of their presence. Mark was never happy at the prospect of anchoring near the beach. The angle of the beach forced the water up into waves that set the boat pitching and tossing, and with no forward momentum it was acutely uncomfortable. Sylvia stood in the swaying galley with hot pans skidding on the gas stove. She had made a stew, although she was feeling more and more queasy. She took her hand from the saucepan handle for one moment, not knowing that a particularly high swell was just about to carry the sloop up and away in a sudden motion. The saucepan, well schooled in Newton's Laws of motion, tried to stay where it was, and the stove moved away from under it. The hot stew fell on to the galley floor and splashed over Sylvia's legs.

'Bloody hell!' she shouted.

Mark was in the cockpit. 'Everything all right?' he called down.

'Yes!' she shouted back, 'I've just spilled the dinner . . . '

Mark appeared in the companionway. 'Never mind. Leave it! There's some chocolate in the starboard locker.'

The night was agony. As the tide turned so the motion of the boat became quicker and more erratic. Sylvia was sick twice. Good sailor though he was, Mark could only keep his chocolate down by great self-control. When dawn broke, they were both relieved to get out of the swaying, tossing saloon and into the fresh air of the deck. They were now far behind schedule, and they had to work very hard with helm and sails to make their best speed along the Kentish coast.

By the time they sailed into Dover harbour in the late afternoon, they were both exhausted. Mark pulled down the sails and took the boat to its mooring on the power of the auxiliary engine. When they were tied up, Sylvia said, 'Mark I must be in work by half past nine tomorrow.'

'Yes. So must I,' he said.

'If I stay down here, that means that I shall have to get up at the crack of dawn to get the train . . . '

Mark looked haggard. 'You want to go back to London tonight?' he asked.

'Would you mind awfully? I'm useless for anything tonight. All I want to do is collapse into bed and sleep the clock around. You'll be coming home next weekend won't you?'

He checked the security of the warps on their cleats and looked up. 'Yes . . . to meet Tim . . . '

Sylvia stood in the companionway and said, 'You don't have to . . . we'll talk over the phone on Monday.'

They both realised as they stepped on to the quay that the trials of the journey had resolved nothing, and a different kind of trial was still to come.

Chapter Eight

Mark looked back over the events of the preceding fortnight with mixed feelings. On the credit side, he had provided a loan for a beautiful woman named Sally Morton to open a second sauna and massage parlour. Her own bank manager had refused – not on financial grounds (the business was booming) – but because as a Methodist lay preacher he suspected he might be giving a fifteen thousand pound encouragement to vice. Mark considered moral judgements by the Bank valid only if they involved direct illegality. He had visited Miss Morton's extant sauna and found it discreet and efficient, but not titillating. This was a cause for minor worry. Had he lost his sexuality somewhere amongst the ledgers and till returns? He felt fit enough, but perhaps his biological drives were subdued by the ache of jealousy he felt when he thought of Sylvia. She was in Brighton with Tim Hart. They were attending the pre-London run of a new play – Sylvia's play, the first she had promoted and shepherded into production.

There was also the unavoidable bankruptcy of one of his clients, a pleasant young garage owner who had lost his licence to carry out M.O.T. inspections. And the Maddox affair still arose in conversations with his Area Manager, who implied that the hustling techniques that had brought Mark success in the International Division might not be appropriate for small-branch management.

The same theme was to arise in conversation with the

Chief General Manager when he came to Dover to speak at the local Institute of Bankers' dinner. It was a disconcerting day for Mark. Sylvia had telephoned to say that she had to stay in Brighton for the Friday night performance of the play; it was the one before last and very important. Consequently she would not be able to attend the dinner with Mark. He felt piqued and betrayed, just as Sylvia felt every time he had missed one of Celia's dinners. His worry about his own handling of the Dover branch's business gnawed at him and Sylvia's absence added to his unease.

As Mark was tying his bow tie, Jenny's father's car drew up outside the cottage. He was used to the young people's flying visits, but on this occasion he was less than delighted to see them, because his taxi was due in fifteen minutes. Jenny wandered off to look at the cliffs, leaving Mark and Peter alone in the small, warm living-room of the cottage.

'Well . . . this is a surprise . . . ' Mark said.

'Not unpleasant, I hope?' Peter asked.

'Of course not . . . did you come down for anything special?'

Peter shook his head. 'Just to ask you for some money for the petrol to drive down here.'

Mark took his dinner jacket from the hanger and slipped it on. As he spoke he checked it over for stray ends of cotton and fluff. 'Is that all?' he asked.

There was a pause before Peter replied. 'Not really,' he said. 'It's just that . . . Mum was strange this morning . . . tense, somehow. Not about anything in particular, just not completely normal . . . and, well things seemed difficult.'

'For you?' Mark asked gently.

Peter was finding it hard to tell his father what was really on his mind. 'No, for the family . . . generally . . . you're down here, we're up there . . . nothing seems to be getting resolved . . . '

Mark poured two sherries and passed one to Peter. 'What did you mean about your mother?' he asked.

Peter's resolve had faltered now he was in the presence of his father. The fine phrases and delicate analysis that he had been rehearsing in his mind during the drive from London evaporated. He muttered several confused things about her probably being unhappy about not being able to come down to Dover that evening, and various other vague phrases.

'So there isn't anything *specific* you're worried about?' Mark asked, very directly.

Peter flushed slightly. 'Is Mum going to come and live here?' he asked.

'I suppose so,' Mark replied. 'I can't imagine us going on like this forever.'

'No,' said Peter, 'I suppose that's what worries me really. That you'll just settle for living apart . . . break up.'

Mark was finding his son's behaviour disturbing. 'Has your mother said anything?' he demanded.

'No!' Peter said very definitely. 'She doesn't even know I'm here. Was it *just* Mum not being able to come with you tonight that upset you?'

'Who said I was upset? '

'No one,' Peter said, his confidence waning again.

There was a long silence. They stood sipping their sherry like early guests at a reception. Mark wanted to say something that would reassure his son. He thought for a moment and continued, 'Look, all I've said is absolutely true. I don't know any reason why we shouldn't all get together soon and . . . well . . . just carry on normally . . . but if anything should happen . . . and I've absolutely no reason to think that anything will . . . you wouldn't be . . . you're security wouldn't be threatened. Both your mother and I would put you first . . . I mean . . . ' Mark, who was usually so articulate, resorted to silence.

'It's all right, Dad, I know that. It's not me I'm thinking about really . . . well not consciously anyway. I mean I've got to look after my ageing Mum and Dad haven't I? Make sure they have enough to eat, and don't upset the Matron of the old folks' home . . . '

There was more communication in their silences than in what they said. Mark drained his sherry. 'Yes,' he said hesitantly. 'Well . . . if we all look after each other, we'll be all right . . . '

Jenny came back in, as tactfully as she had left. Mark remembered the petrol money and took a five pound note from his wallet. Then he took out another two and held them out to Peter. 'Look,' he said, 'go and have a good meal and a nice evening . . . '

Peter protested, but finally took the money.

'Come on then,' he said to Jenny. 'Let's find a Bistro with soft lights and sweet music . . . see you then, dad.'

'Yes,' Mark said quietly. 'Drive carefully.'

'I will, don't worry,' Jenny said, and they headed for the door.

Mark stood watching them out of the window. The car went down the gravel drive, flashed its indicator for a right turn, and the two youngsters waved before they disappeared up the Dover road.

Mark looked at his hand and realised it was trembling. He went to the sideboard, took out a bottle of Scotch, and poured himself a large drink.

He looked at the telephone, went across to it, and dialed the Brighton hotel where Sylvia was staying. There was no reply from her room.

The dinner, like most dinners, was a mixture of rich food, heavy wine, and heavier jokes. Mark was glad when it was over. He was conversing only with the top of his mind. The burden of his thoughts was far away.

Harvey had agreed to spend the night in the cottage and return to London the following morning. He had been very restrained in his drinking during the dinner but was now glad to clutch a large glass of whisky in his hand.

'Don't want them to say that the Chief General Manager was really putting it away at dinner tonight,' he said.

They settled by the fire. 'Good speech,' Mark observed.

'It was all right, I suppose,' said Harvey, who gave it on average once a week. 'It went down better in Dorset though. I was there last night.'

'I thought it was very good,' said Mark. 'There's a lot of apprehension amongst managers. Everything's changing so fast. It's obvious to everyone that the local branches have to be cut down. Everybody's hoping it will be someone else that feels the edge . . . '

'It's the same in every industry in Britain. Unions demand more pay – and quite rightly – to keep up with inflation. The only way the employer can agree is to increase efficiency – that is to do the same work with less men. Increase unemployment.'

Mark nodded. 'But the banks have managed to avoid confrontation with their workers,' he said.

'Well we can afford to take a longer view – that's all. We have enough fat to be able to slide into changes. In a merger, keep on both managers until one retires. That sort of thing. British Rail or British Leyland don't have that sort of fat.'

'No,' said Mark, 'but I must say how grateful I was that you were able to accept the invitation at such short notice. Put up my stock locally no end . . . '

Harvey smiled over the whisky. 'You don't need that surely, Mark? You must be a very big fish in this pond. When are you going to be ready to leave it?'

This was a subject that Mark had been hoping to avoid. 'I thought we'd been through all that when I decided to move in the first place.'

Harvey could not agree. 'No Mark,' he said, 'we didn't. You were very tired. You'd had a hard couple of years. We felt you had deserved a break, especially after the Manton's coup . . . do you know by the way, they approached us about financing a factory in Yorkshire?'

Mark nodded. 'I did hear a whisper . . . '

'It's true,' Harvey continued, 'and I think we'll get it. It's down to you, and we were grateful and gave you a sabbatical . . . '

Mark launched an interruption but Harvey waved it aside. 'No, Mark. You listen. We gave you a sabbatical to come to your own realisation . . . but we feel it's gone on long enough.'

Mark was shaken. 'A few months? That's ridiculous. In any case when I asked for this job, I told you if I didn't get it, or an equivalent one, I'd resign. Well the same thing still goes.'

There was a pause. Harvey swilled the Scotch around in his glass and then said, 'I should be careful, if I were you. If you do say that again, I would be inclined to accept your resignation.'

This was not what Mark had expected to hear. He had reconciled himself to continual requests for him to return to the International Division. But this . . . ?

'But you were saying just now that I deserve something from the Bank for the Manton's deal . . . '

Harvey nodded. 'We gave you a break.'

'But it's ridiculous,' Mark found himself saying too loudly. He calmed his voice. 'If I'm that good, what possible point would there be in getting rid of me – just to justify a theoretical position on promotion . . . ?'

'It's not just theoretical. This would be a practical, common sense decision. I said you were a good international banker. I didn't say you were a good branch manager. As a matter of fact I don't think you are very good in that job.'

'But how can you say that?' Mark stuttered.

'You want me to justify it?'

Harvey waited for Mark's answer.

'Yes, I do.'

'All right. Let's start with Maddox Engineering. You're aware you didn't cover yourself in glory on that job. You panicked Maddox into the market and triggered his own take-over bid.'

Mark leaned forward and vented some of his irritation on a log that was lying too near the front of the grate. 'I see,' he said. 'You've been spying on me!'

'For goodness' sake, Mark! You manage your branch, the Regional Director manages you and I manage the Regional Director. You know what your Assistant Manager is doing, don't you?'

Mark sat back in his chair. 'Yes . . . I'm sorry. That was a stupid thing to say.'

Harvey nodded again. 'Right,' he said. 'Look Mark, we watched you very closely, not because we don't respect you, but because we do. Just because you were a good branch manager once doesn't automatically mean you can go back and do it again. I couldn't. I'm damn sure I couldn't. I know you know all there is to know but the edge isn't there. It can't be. You've moved too long in a different world. "You can't go back" isn't just a theoretical statement. It reflects a reality.'

This seemed to Mark terribly unfair. 'I made one mistake . . . ' he began.

'You realise it *was* a mistake, then?'

'Well, if I had to do it again I'd handle it differently, I suppose.'

Again Harvey nodded. 'Right,' he said again, 'and your decision over Hetherington, that farmer chap with his caravan idea or whatever, wasn't brilliant. I would have been happier if you'd got him to rationalise his position more. It wasn't a stupid decision . . . but honestly from where I stand can't you see I might think you were . . . not quite rigorous enough?'

Harvey held his whisky glass out and Mark poured some more for him, freshening his own glass at the same time. 'Tom Stetchley wanted me to lend and he was the most conservative banker I ever knew,' said Mark.

'I don't know what he was like when he was younger. All I know is we accepted *his* resignation.'

There was a long pause before Mark said, 'I see.'

Harvey's voice changed from managerial lecture to a more sympathetic note. 'Mark I haven't come down here to beat you into the ground. I came down here to convince you that the bank regards you as a first class man with just the experience we require for a position opening up in the International Division.'

'And if I refuse to take it?' Mark asked steadily.

Harvey kept his voice low. 'I didn't come down here to threaten you either. If I can be sure you're thinking clearly about yourself and your qualities, which the bank values, I'll be happy. So let's leave it shall we? We both need to think . . . '

There was another long pause. 'If that's what you want,' Mark said.

'What I want is to finish my drink and get off up to bed. I have to set off by nine in the morning. The car's picking me up. By the way is Sylvia coming down tomorrow?'

'Er . . . no . . . ' said Mark, stumbling over his words.

'So you'll be going up to town. Excellent . . . we can travel up together . . . ' said Harvey, and swilled the last of the whisky before standing up.

Tim and Sylvia walked slowly along the corridor.

'That was a very nice evening Tim,' she said.

She turned towards her door. Tim kept his hand on the frame.

'A night cap?' he asked.

'No, thank you.'

He removed his hand and said with a sigh, 'Ah! . . . Well, I promised I wouldn't twist your arm.'

'I'm very tired,' she said and put the key into the lock. She kissed him gently on the cheek and opened the door.

'Good-night,' he said, and walked slowly away up the corridor to his room.

Sylvia went inside and closed the door after her.

Tim hung his jacket on a hanger and sat on the bed to take his shoes off. He had been making gentle advances to Sylvia for what seemed like a very long time now. Really, he thought to himself, this has gone far enough. She seems to be enjoying it, but if it goes sour I shall not only lose a friend, I shall also lose a very useful partner in the office.

He leaned over and switched on the bed-side lamp, and walked over to the door and switched off the main light. He had just undressed when there was a tap on his door. He reached out, slipped on his dressing-gown, and went to answer it.

Sylvia stood in the corridor wearing a robe over her nightdress. She held a bottle of champagne and two glasses.

Tim reacted as quickly as he could, although he was extremely surprised. 'Come in . . . ' he said.

'Thank you,' she said. She came into the room, walked across to the table and put down the glasses. She began to tear the foil off the champagne.

'This is a surprise,' said Tim and meant it.

She looked across at him and smiled. She said nothing, but began untwisting the wire on the bottle. The cork shot out and ricocheted off the ceiling. The champagne streamed out of the bottle as she tried to catch it in the glasses.

She passed him a glass, held hers up and said, 'Cheers!'

'Cheers!'

They stood sipping the champagne. 'I thought you didn't want a night cap,' Tim observed gently.

'What I didn't want, above all, was a seduction.'

Tim laughed and sipped his champagne. 'Of you . . . or

me? I mean, coming to my room – and me only half dressed . . . if I'm not careful you'll have me in bed before I know where I am . . . '

She was serious. 'If we were going to make love, Tim, it had to be because of a decision, not a bungling half-hearted spur of the moment whim.'

Tim moved closer to her. 'And are we going to make love?'

She sipped the champagne. 'Well I am . . . you're very welcome to join in.'

Holding his champagne carefully away from her blue dressing-gown he leaned forward and kissed her. It began as a soft touching of lips, but as she moved to him it gathered the passion that they had been holding away from themselves for so long.

When they pulled apart to take breath Tim said, 'You're a strange woman.'

'Really? Have I put you off your stroke?'

'No.'

'I'm glad.'

Tim was shaking his head with the wonder of it. 'So, you go to your room, order the champagne, dress in your most provocative nightie and come along.'

She shook her head. 'No . . . the champagne was already there . . . I bought it at the off licence on the way . . . you don't think I was going to pay hotel prices do you? I wasn't brought up a Scot for nothing!'

'So you knew all evening that you were going to . . . take advantage of me?'

'Yes.'

Tim was smiling and shaking his head at the same time as though he had invented something miraculous and wasn't quite sure how it worked.

'I don't like seductions, Tim,' Sylvia went on. 'They're a real put-down – usually by the woman herself. It's mostly a mechanism for coping with guilt – but once you realise that, it won't work anyway, so why persist with the game?'

Tim put his hands on her shoulders. 'And you don't feel guilt.'

'Oh I do!'

'So how will you cope with it?'

'I don't know.'

'But you'll risk it?'

She touched his face. 'If you will,' she said.

Tim heaped amazement on amazement. 'Me?'

'Yes, you,' she insisted. 'I don't know about tomorrow. I just know it will come. I don't know what I'll feel about Mark. Obviously I'll feel something. Maybe I'll have to leave Tim Hart Productions. Maybe I'll have to leave Mark. All I can promise is that I won't feel you'll have to make an honest woman of me. There are no strings as far as you're concerned.'

Tim kissed the tip of her nose. 'And what if I wanted to make an honest woman of you?' he asked softly and kissed her nose again.

She shrugged. 'All that belongs to tomorrow.'

Tim took her now empty glass and set it down on the table together with his. He came close to her and kissed her on the mouth. Her lips opened, and her hips came forward to press against his. He put his arms around her and pulled her even closer in the kiss. Then he pulled his head back and said, 'Just one more thing?'

'Yes?' she said, pulling at the belt of his dressing-gown.

'If it's Tim Hart Productions you decide to leave, I'll put up a hell of a fight.'

Sylvia opened her dressing-gown and let it fall to the carpet. She stood for a moment in her nightdress – which, gently enhanced her soft, fair beauty. Then his fingers slipped the shoulder straps down over her arms and the nightdress fell away.

In a second they were naked in each others arms, and then he held her hand and led her to the bed.

Their love-making was new and exciting. Technically, it might have been faulted, but technique was much less important to them than the joy that set them giggling and laughing and kissing in each others arms. Sylvia was surprised at how different it could be to feel the touch of another man's body on hers. She had become accustomed to Mark – more than she had realised – and accustomed to their love-making being a set of variations on the same theme. With Tim it was fresh, unfamiliar. It was actually easier to make love than it had been *not* to make love.

Afterwards they lay calmly entwined on the bed. Sylvia

turned her head and looked at Tim. 'There had to be a resolution,' she said. 'One way or another. Before, it was all sex in the head, and more important things ought to be going on there.'

Tim tweaked her nose again. 'Well, I'm glad I've released you for a more important activity,' he said.

Sylvia realised what she had said. 'Oh Tim. I didn't mean that . . . you know I didn't.'

'I know,' he said softly. 'I was teasing . . . do you know what you'll do about tomorrow?'

'About Mark . . . ? No, not yet.'

'I meant what I said about fighting you leaving.'

Their faces were very close. 'I know,' she said. 'Tim, let's let tomorrow look after itself, shall we?'

He smiled. 'Willingly,' he said.

He ran his fingers down the small of her back, and drew her to him again.

Mark did not enjoy his drive back to London with Harvey. Not once did they speak of his defection from the International Division, but the thought of it soured the fine morning. He was glad to reach Islington and the empty house. He put some coffee on to percolate.

It was erupting like a muddy volcano in the top of the Cona when Peter came in. 'I didn't know you were coming home,' he said.

Mark explained about the lift with Harvey.

'Hey, Dad,' said Peter. 'We had a smashing dinner last night . . . in Canterbury. Thank you.'

'That's all right,' said Mark.

Sylvia came in just as Mark was pouring out the coffee. She was plainly surprised and disconcerted to see Mark. 'Oh . . . hello . . . how was the dinner?' she asked.

'Predictable,' said Mark.

'And Harvey?'

Mark laughed. 'Unpredictable.'

Sylvia waited for him to continue.

'We had a bit of a set-to at the cottage afterwards . . . it seems they're leaning on me to come back,' Mark explained as he poured out an extra cup of coffee for Sylvia.

'Can they force you, Dad?' asked Peter.

'Well,' said Mark, 'we don't have direction of labour yet . . . but . . . yes I suppose they could if they really made up their minds.'

Peter smiled. 'So we won't have to go down to Dover after all . . . Sorry, Dad that wasn't very tactful.'

Mark turned to Sylvia. 'And how was your night?'

'Oh . . . very exciting. The play was good.'

Mark light a cigarette. 'And how was Tim?' he asked.

'Tim?' Sylvia might never have heard of him.

'Look I've got to get a book from Jeremy . . . what time's lunch, Mum?' Peter asked.

'Usual time,' she said. 'One o'clock I suppose.'

Peter paused in the doorway. 'You'll both be here then?'

They nodded, and their son backed out of the room feeling very embarrassed.

Mark and Sylvia looked at each other for a few moments. 'He's worried about something. Do you know what it is?' Mark asked her.

'Us, I suppose.'

'Has he any reason to worry?'

At his question Sylvia dropped her head and looked into the cup for convenient, safe answers.

'Yes,' she said.

Mark examined her face, and knew what was written there.

'Tim Hart?' he asked, after a time.

Sylvia felt herself breathing only with the very top of her lungs. 'I slept with him last night . . . it was the first time.'

Her words seemed to release a pent-up surge of energy and emotion in Mark, as he stood up from his chair, knocking his coffee over the table and rushed out of the kitchen.

Sylvia righted the cup and tried to control her breathing. She poured more coffee for both of them and carried it through to the living-room.

He was sitting motionless, in the armchair by the piano. The energy of his bolt from the kitchen had gone. He trembled after the blow like a diving-board after the leap of the diver.

She put the coffee on the small table beside him.

'Are you leaving me?' he asked.

He looked up and followed the question with a sad, accusing gaze.

Sylvia's chest tightened again under the bands of that stare, but she said, 'If you ask me to.'

'And if I don't?'

'I'd like time to think. To talk with you. To try to understand what's happening. To try to make a calm decision.'

Something in the anaesthetic way she issued this stay of execution released another strained rope of bitterness.

'Well... was he good?' he demanded.

'Mark!'

Again, the outburst discharged, he sank back into himself.

'I'm sorry. That was cheap,' he said, and turned his head away from her. And then, 'I shan't ask you to go.'

Sylvia was quite still, her eyes heavy with the terrible concentration it demanded, this dangerous forcing of the issue. 'Thank you,' she said simply.

When he turned his face back to her, the anger and resentment had been moulded into a new expression; a sad smile of self-recognition. There was no special pleading in his voice, but the shock of finding a new perspective from which he seemed smaller.

'It seems I only have to offer to resign and everyone falls over themselves to accept it...' he said.

Sylvia burst into tears. It was sudden and uncontrollable; violent tears and the need to be sick. She ran from the room and fled upstairs.

Mark walked slowly to the drinks cabinet and poured himself a very large brandy.

Chapter Nine

The following Monday morning, Mark marched into Harvey's office and demanded to know exactly what was going on.

'I have no intention of fighting with you, Mark, however belligerently you behave. Sit down and have some coffee,' the Chief General Manager insisted.

Mark apologised. 'That's all right,' said Harvey. 'Now, take off your boxing gloves.'

Harvey interrogated Mark closely about his time in Dover. Was he really happy? Had it come up to his expectations?

Mark was hesitant in his answers. Harvey skilfully exploited that hesitation. He compared Mark's qualified replies with the great expectations he had proclaimed in this very office when he left the International Division.

'We didn't replace you when you left, and we've also had a retirement,' Harvey continued. 'We're under-strength, and we want you back – not to fill a gap – but because you have the languages and the feel for international business . . . But it wouldn't be your old job. Philip Haslet is going to be concentrating on developing our South American business. We're pretty weak there and there's a tremendous potential. We want you to be his deputy with special responsibility for Europe. It will be pretty much your own show. We would give you a personal assistant – one of the new graduates. We're finding ways of bringing them into the higher echelons of the bank.'

Mark smiled. 'And you think this an offer I can't refuse,' he said.

'If you do refuse,' continued Harvey, 'it will only prove that we were wrong to offer it . . . if you don't jump at the chance it will show that your . . . malaise . . . was not a temporary aberration, but a serious end to your career.'

Harvey sat back and snapped a biscuit between his fingers.

'So . . . you will take away the Dover job if I refuse?' Mark asked.

'I'm not making threats, Mark. I'm telling you about the attitudes of my management team. Don't you think you ought to go back and consider it before you make any decisions? Why don't you take a day or two off. Really talk it over with Sylvia. I'm sure she'll want you back in London.'

Mark shook his head firmly. 'No . . . I've got things to do in Dover,' he said.

Harvey stood up, the interview was at an end. 'We need to know by next Monday.'

Mark remained in his chair. 'That's quick,' he complained.

'Monday.'

Three miles away in Shaftesbury Avenue, Sylvia was telling Tim of her bald, traumatic admission to Mark of what had happened.

'There isn't a good way to tell a husband you've made love to another man,' he said.

'I didn't mean that. Friday night was marvellous. But I wanted to get clear in my head on what level it was marvellous . . . I'm not sixteen, Tim. I don't have to try to convince myself that if I've enjoyed lovemaking, I must be head over heels in love with the fellow . . . And I still haven't got it clear now.'

'I have . . . I love you, Sylvia,' he said without a trace of sentimentality.

'Too easy, Tim.'

'It damn well isn't! I've guarded my independence pretty carefully over the years . . . '

She sat down at her desk. 'I'm sorry,' she said. 'I suppose what I meant was that it would be too easy for me to say the same thing.'

Tim reverted to his usual extravagant manner. 'Go on! Say it! This is the last office in London that would countenance any kind of censorship . . . '

'No Tim,' she said, aware of how much easier this conversation was than her clash with Mark. 'I was brought up to spend things very carefully. Especially words. I know the word love can be used freely – but if ever I tell you I love you, then I'm afraid you'll have lost your carefully guarded independence.'

He smiled. 'I'll look forward to that.'

'Don't count on it,' she said. 'Now shall we start work?'

Tim nodded and returned to his office. There was a great deal to be done. The London opening of their Brighton play was on Wednesday, and the programmes had not yet arrived.

Sylvia was arguing on the telephone with the printers when she had another visitor. Peter tapped on the door and walked into the room.

'What are you doing here?' she asked, after a quiet visual check for signs of illness.

'Just thought I'd drop in,' he said.

'But what about school? You can't afford to stay off like this!'

He sat on the edge of her desk. 'I can't afford weekends like we've just had, either. What was it all about?'

She thought quickly and suppressed her feeling that she should be honest with her son. 'I can't tell you, Peter,' she said.

'That's the problem, isn't it? Nobody was saying anything to anybody all weekend. It was like living in a home for deaf-mutes. What's likely to happen?'

She put her hand on his arm. 'Nothing is likely to happen – at least for some time,' she said. 'There's no urgency.'

He snorted. 'That's *your* opinion . . . so you're not going to discuss it with me?'

'I don't feel I can Peter. Not until the weekend, when I can talk it over with your father.'

He shrugged and made for the door.

'Where are you going?' Sylvia asked.

'Back to school. I've always done what I'm told, haven't I? Don't worry. I'm not going to jump in the river!'

'Peter!'

He smiled at her, and went out, crashing the door behind him.

On the way back to Dover Mark met Maddox on the train. He made no reference to the take-over bid, except to say that Christopher now lived in Belgravia on the proceeds from his shares.

'I'm sorry,' said Mark.

Maddox brushed it aside with his characteristic bluntness. He was not a man to bear a grudge; except possibly against Christopher. 'Wasn't your fault,' he said. 'The prodigal son . . . The only difference is that when he comes home broke, I'll feed *him* to the fatted calf!'

Maddox had been to Oxford to see his younger son, who was reading Engineering at the University. Any affection that he had withdrawn from the elder son's account had now been banked with the younger.

'Always promised myself,' Maddox continued, 'that once I got rid of the work. I'd have time to do all the things I haven't had time for before. Now I'm doing them. But there's a funny thing; when your relationships are squeezed into the cracks of a heavy work programme, they're golden. They're the cement that keeps the wall of your life together. But when they become the whole wall . . . do you realise how weak a cement wall is?'

Maddox left the question in the air and walked on to his seat.

Carol and Keith were glowing with health after a weekend working together on an archaeological dig. When Mark arrived at the bank they were standing in his office arguing the future of the local branches of Knight's Bank. Mark, too, was looking stronger than he had seemed for weeks, and when he asked questions about the diary and issued instructions to them, he had some of the quickness of decision he had originally brought to Dover and then lost.

He sent Carol out to buy all the theatre newspapers and journals. She was surprised, but made no comment. He asked Keith for an up-to-date assessment of the financial decisions that must be taken. How, for example, does one finance an electronics wizard with no security but his intellectual brilliance, and the business sense of a three year old aboriginal?

It was later in the day before Mark telephoned Maddox and asked him if he would consider being the business consultant for a small but unique electronics firm that needed an experienced hand on the tiller. Maddox was delighted. Since he had refused to 'lick stamps' for Western Foundries he had in truth been his own prodigal, wandering from pleasure to pleasure ill-equipped for such a rich diet without a leavening crust of work.

Then Mark phoned Sylvia. 'Your first night on Wednesday,' he said. 'I've changed my mind. I'm coming after all. I may be late for the performance but I'll be there for the party. I'm still invited I hope?'

'Of course,' she said.

'Good. Tell Tim I'm looking forward to meeting him.' There was silence on the line, then Sylvia asked, 'Are you sure you're all right, Mark?'

He was definite. 'Absolutely. I'm alive and kicking. Now I can't stop. I'm very busy. Don't worry about Peter, I'll give him a ring tonight.'

Mark rang off, leaving Sylvia puzzled.

Mark was, in contrast, barely surprised when Peter announced himself at the counter. Sylvia had told him about his son's arrival at her office. It was 12.30, so Mark took Peter off immediately to the Yacht Club for lunch.

'Now, I gather you're on a tour of disaffected parents,' Mark said briskly, as they stood at the bar. 'Well Peter, I'm not going to tell you anything either – for exactly the same reasons as your mother. But I will say one thing. Of course it could happen that your mother and I could be split up . . . one of us could die or find someone else.

There's no certainty in this world . . . and you're old enough to realise that. But this I *can* promise you. I have no intention of leaving home, and neither has your mother at this moment. I shall do everything I can to make sure she won't want to.'

'Does that mean . . . ?' Peter interrupted.

'What it says,' Mark continued. 'Neither more nor less. I could have said that at any time during our nineteen years of marriage – give or take a few months.'

Peter toyed with his glass of lager. 'These last few months?' he asked.

Mark shrugged. 'Shall we say I've been preoccupied.'

'What with?'

'Myself?'

Tim and Sylvia were lunching in the office as they finished plans for the opening night and the party which was to follow.

'It's nineteen years' investment,' Sylvia was saying, 'the sweat, the effort, the suffering, the laughing. It's not easy to throw all that away.'

Tim poured out some wine. 'I'm not pressing you, Sylvia . . . But don't persist in thinking it's kindness. It isn't. I'm acting in my own best interests. I'm doing everything I can to make sure I win you in the end.'

She smiled and shook her head at the cleverness of the man. He could turn a confession of selfishness into a declaration of love.

'If I'm to break my marriage,' she said, 'I'll break it in the same way as I came to your room. With forethought. I'm not going to crumble into a decision, wining, dining, loving with you. Nor am I going to provoke Mark into breaking it. I shall wait for Wednesday at least.'

'What's magic about Wednesday, apart from the first night?'

'Mark's coming. I want to talk to him.'

'You did that this weekend,' he said. He was watching her closely now, the bottle still in his hand.

'No,' she said. 'We talked *at* each other, when we talked at all.'

He put the bottle back on to her desk beside the plate of sandwiches.

'And after Wednesday?' he enquired.

'We'll just have to see . . .'

Chapter Ten

Rapturous applause filled the London theatre on Wednesday evening, but the notices would not be in the morning papers for a few hours yet. The audience had gone, and the curtain had risen again for the party. The movables had been struck from the stage, but the cast and their guests danced in and around the set.

Jenny and Peter were among the dancers excited by the presence of so many celebrities. Celia danced with Max, who was full of charming compliments to Sylvia's good taste in choosing and mounting the play.

Sylvia, wearing the dress she had bought on the day she was offered the job, stood by Tim and refused to dance with him.

Mark had still not arrived.

She insisted they circulate. With a bottle of champagne in each hand Sylvia moved among the cast, congratulating here, joking there.

'Recharge your glasses?' she asked Max and Celia when she found herself beside them.

'I will if I'm allowed to toast my protégé,' Max said. 'Remember I suggested this job!'

She kissed him on the cheek and gave him an awkward hug.

'I arrive at the party to find my wife in the arms of another man!' said a familiar voice behind her.

Mark was wearing a dinner jacket. He was carefully groomed and smiling broadly.

'Mark,' Sylvia exclaimed, 'I didn't see you arrive.'

'Well, you'll have to be more careful,' he said laughing.

He kissed Sylvia, and then Celia, and shook hands warmly with Max. Peter and Jenny forced their way through the crowd to them.

'Hello Peter, hello Jenny,' Mark said. 'Having a good evening?'

Jenny was very excited. 'Oh great,' she said. 'You should have seen the play.'

'I will soon, I promise you . . . I'm sorry darling,' he directed to Sylvia, 'I had to go to the Regional Office. It was important. Then I had to go home to change into this.' He gestured disparagingly down at his formal attire.

'Did it go well?' Sylvia asked. 'The Regional Office?'

'Perfectly. We were arranging a new job for Maddox – the man who fell to a take-over bid . . . Still, no banking tonight. It's *your* night. It seems to have been a great success.'

'It was,' said Max.

'It still is darling,' Celia's rich voice boomed over the loud disco music. 'Look at her. She's as smug as a dog with two tails.'

Mark glanced at Sylvia. 'And why shouldn't she be smug. She has two tails: a family and a job she likes. And I can tell you, the going may get rough on occasion, but the combination takes some beating . . . Isn't that true?'

The question was directed at Sylvia. 'Yes . . . It is,' she said. She could see Tim approaching. Mark followed her gaze and saw for the first time the man whose name was so familiar. There was intelligence and strength of will in the eyes. *Perhaps I could like you*, Mark thought.

They shook hands formally – two intelligent men with strength of will – aware of the attention focused on them.

'I'm delighted to meet you,' said Tim.

'Yes, the feeling's reciprocated. I have a great deal to thank you for . . . Sylvia's happiness, a successful evening and a good show I gather.'

Tim's shoulders relaxed, just a little. 'Yes, I was very pleased. I'm looking forward to the reviews in the morning much more than I usually do. It's our occupational hazard. I don't think anyone else but show business people have to suffer judgement as we do.'

Mark frowned. 'I don't know. Surely we all do in different ways. True, your judgement comes swiftly, but if I made a bad lending decision the judgement is just as sure – even if it is delayed.'

'But not so public,' said Tim.

'Some bankruptcies are pretty public,' Mark replied, and went on to elaborate the point.

Sylvia was tense, holding down her nervousness under a cheerful smile. *I know both these men*, she thought. *I have felt them both pull at my life. I cannot believe they are standing here talking to each other like this.*

' . . . I shall see it very soon,' Mark was saying.

'Well, as soon as you can get up from the sticks, just give us a ring. We always keep house seats for the last minute V.I.P.'

Mark smiled his thanks. 'That's kind . . . but actually I shall be living up here again, very soon.'

Sylvia stepped forward. 'Mark! You're leaving Dover?'

'I'm afraid so darling. All our plans, for a lovely house and sailing and so on, dished!'

Mark outlined the details of his return, and his new position as Deputy to the Manager of the Foreign Division in charge of European operations.

'So you'll still have to travel a lot,' Sylvia observed.

'Quite a bit, but not as much as before. I shall have assistants to do the heavy leg-work.'

Tim Hart reached over to Sylvia and took one of the champagne bottles. 'Well, congratulations are in order then,' he said. He tried to pour from it but it was empty. 'The Head Office still wants you back?' he asked Mark.

'Indeed. They made me an offer I couldn't refuse.'

'That's an ominous phrase,' Tim commented. 'So it wasn't a completely free decision?'

Mark frowned again. 'Is there such a thing? Marx said freedom was the recognition of necessity. I'm too convinced a capitalist, I suppose, to believe everything he said, but there's a lot of truth in that phrase.'

Tim said that he liked to think of himself as a free agent.

'Of course,' Mark replied, 'so do we all. But it's amazing, isn't it, how often, when we are most free, we look for some bonds to make us secure? Don't you find that?'

Tim appealed to the company. 'Oh, give this man some

champagne, please. It's not fair. He's stone cold sober and we're half-cut!'

Sylvia had not realised that Mark had no drink. She gave him her glass and went to fetch another.

Mark looked at Tim and held up the glass. 'Well,' he said, 'a toast then . . . to the show and its manager.'

'I'll drink to that,' called Tim.

Sylvia returned in time to hear the toast in her honour. 'Speech, speech,' Celia insisted, and the others took up her cry.

After much protest, Sylvia prepared herself. She was looking at Mark, forcing him to take the full meaning of her words. 'I'd like to propose a toast in reply,' she began. 'I propose we drink to the performance we've seen tonight. It's not easy coming before an audience, some of them apathetic, some even hostile, and giving a performance that sparkles and is completely convincing. It takes courage and love . . . Even though it is mixed with a little fear. Well, tonight's performance was superb. I drink to it.'

She lifted her glass and drank, amid cheers and cries of 'Hear! hear!' After the toast, the party swung easily back to its chatter and exuberance.

Sylvia came nearer to Mark. 'Well, I think I ought to be taking Peter and Jenny home,' he said. There were many cries of protest. 'Yes really!' he continued. 'Darling, would you forgive me? It has been a hell of a day. I know I've only been here a moment, but . . . '

'I'll come with you,' Sylvia interrupted.

He would have none of it. 'Please stay,' he said. 'This is your night. You did it on your own. Enjoy it that way. I'll be at home.'

Peter began an objection to such an early departure, but Mark took his arm firmly and led him a few paces away.

'What's all this about, Dad?' Peter demanded. 'Why are we leaving Mum?'

'Peter,' Mark replied, 'I think you already *know* what this is all about. Or at least you're bright enough to guess. There's an old banker's adage. Always sell on a rising market. Or as a professional gambler would put it, always quit when you're ahead.'

Peter grinned at his father, and took Jenny's hand. The

three of them said their good-byes and walked away through the wings.

Tim and Sylvia stood, watching them go.

'Well,' said Tim. 'If one has to lose, at least it's good to lose to a worthy opponent . . . a man of style.'

'Yes,' said Sylvia firmly, 'he is that.'

'At least may I have the last waltz?'

She turned to him. He took her in his arms, and they danced.

Mark sat at the piano, playing a lingering melody. A glass of whisky stood beside the scrolled music stand on the piano. His jacket and bow-tie lay over the arm of the settee.

Sylvia let herself into the house quietly and came into the sitting room. Mark stopped playing at once.

'Don't stop!' she protested.

'I want to. Let me get you a drink.'

She breathed out expansively. 'I think I've had enough . . . All right, perhaps a small one . . . But not too much grain with the grape.'

He reached down beside the piano stool and lifted a bottle of champagne. 'I wasn't thinking of whisky,' he said. He removed the cork in one swift practised motion.

'More champagne?' Sylvia asked. 'I shall float up in the air with all these bubbles.'

'That's what I'm counting on,' he grinned. 'I'm up there already. Besides, not even Tim Hart Productions could afford this vintage!'

Mark poured out the champagne. Sylvia shook her head with disbelief. 'Oh Mark,' she said, 'You are the most completely unpredictable man I have ever met!'

'What did you think I was going to do. Have a fight?'

She nodded. 'You did, didn't you?'

He pulled a face. 'Oh really! Was that how it struck you?'

Sylvia sipped her champagne, never taking her eyes from Mark's. 'Tim was most impressed. He said if one had to lose it was better to lose to a worthy opponent.'

Mark nodded. 'That's true,' he agreed.

'You don't mind my mentioning him, do you?' she

added, apparently as an afterthought.

'Why should I? He's your employer, isn't he? Imagine you will talk about him from time to time . . . At least until you get another job.'

Her smile dimmed a little. 'I see. That may not be for a while. There aren't that many jobs.'

Mark lifted his glass. 'We can wait. Can't we?'

Sylvia nodded. 'I can.'

'So can I.'

'And you're really coming back to London?'

'Yes,' said Mark. 'I'm sorry I've given you such a hard time.'

She took his hand. 'I had my . . . revenge . . . I wish it didn't seem so . . . cheap now.'

'It doesn't seem that way to me.'

'Really?'

'Really.'

She pulled him towards the door. 'Don't you think we can take these glasses up to bed?'

He allowed himself to be drawn gently across the room, and into the hall.

'I'm glad you made it to the party,' Sylvia said, as they set foot on the stairs. 'I'm so glad . . . but you came just in time, the exact moment . . . Did you have to rush? How long did you have to change?'

Mark paused on the half-landing and pretended to calculate it in his mind. 'Oh . . . I'd say about . . . two and a half hours.'

Sylvia turned to him laughing and kissed his hand.

'Oh!' she said, 'Oh . . . Mark Telford . . . You clever sod!'

They stood for a moment grinning at each other, and then climbed up the last six stairs to bed.

THE END

THE GREEK TYCOON by EILEEN LOTTMAN

The romance that stunned the world . . . He had money enough to buy everything, and what he couldn't buy with money, he captured with charm.

He was a man who gloried in gambling for ships, for power and for the love of the most sought after woman in the world.

0 552 10888 X - 85p

THE DOCTOR'S WIFE by BRIAN MOORE

'Nightmare images of tanks cruising down empty night streets, feverish erotic couplings with a stranger in foreign hotels; a married woman with one son from a provincial backwater breaking out on a trip abroad; a concerned sibling observing a rebellious young sister; the palpable absence of God in the central characters' lives and the notion that art and sex might replace Him . . . the principal ingredients of Brian Moore's fine new novel . . . a splendidly bracing experience.' NEW STATESMAN

'The most alluringly complex adulteress to come along in print for some time.' TIME MAGAZINE

0 552 10761 1 - 85p